William Shakespeare's Love's Labor's Lost: A Retelling in Prose

David Bruce

Published by David Bruce, 2022.

Table of Contents

Dedication

Dedicated to My Uncle Reuben Saturday

When he was a young man, my mother's brother Reuben wanted to escape from poverty and lard sandwiches, so he tried to run away from it. He stole a car so he could drive up north where he hoped to find opportunity, but he got caught and ended up on a Georgia chain gang for several months. In a chain gang, prisoners are shackled every few feet by the ankles to a long length of chain to keep them from escaping. They work in the hot sun while shackled to the chain, and when they sleep, they are shackled to the bed. No freedom, hard work, hot sun, no pay, bad food, and some mean guards.

When my uncle got released from the chain gang, he hitchhiked up north. He did what a lot of people trying to escape from poverty do: He drifted. He drifted from town to town, seeking opportunity and not finding it. He worked when he could, but the jobs were temporary and low pay. My uncle slept rough often, and he was hungry often. Once, when he was completely broke and completely hungry, he saw a restaurant with a buffet and went inside and asked to speak to the manager. He said, "I am very hungry, I don't have any money, and I would appreciate it very much if you would give me any food that the restaurant is going to throw away. I will be happy to wait by the rear entrance until you are ready to throw away food."

The manager told him to sit down at a table, and then the manager went to the buffet, loaded a big plate high with food, and gave it to him free of charge.

One way out of poverty is to get a good job, and my uncle got out of poverty by getting a job working with sheet metal.

My uncle's work ethic helped him. His employer sent him to California to do some special sheet-metal work, and the people in California wanted to keep him there. They explained that their California employees liked to come to work late, leave early, and take many days off. It was difficult to get someone who would show up and do the work they were supposed to do and were paid to do.

My uncle was also good with money. He got married, bought a house, and raised six children. Each time he made a mortgage payment, he paid extra money so he could pay off the mortgage faster.

If there was a sale on food, he bought lots of it. For example, if there was a sale on peanut butter, two jars for the price of one, he would buy twelve jars and sometimes go back the next day and buy six more jars.

If you went in his pantry — a closet set aside to store food — you saw that it was packed with food. If you went in his kitchen, you saw that he had taken off the doors of the high cabinets in which he stored food so that he could see the food. If you went in his bedroom, you saw that he had all the regular bedroom furniture, but he also had lots of shelves he had installed. The shelves were loaded with things that he had bought on sale that he knew his family could use: food (of course), light bulbs, toothpaste, toilet paper, etc. His bedroom looked like a warehouse.

Once he made a bad purchase: he bought a case of baked beans. Beans are beans, but the sauce they came in can taste good or bad, and the sauce these beans came in tasted bad. His kids told him, "Dad, throw those beans away! They're awful!"

But when you grow up poor, you don't throw beans away. For a long time, whenever my uncle and his family ate baked beans, they ate a mixture of one can of good baked beans and one can of bad baked beans.

My uncle's kids never had to eat lard sandwiches.

***

The doing of good deeds is important. As a free person, you can choose to live your life as a good person or as a bad person. To be a good person, do good deeds. To be a bad person, do bad deeds. If you do good deeds, you will become good. If you do bad deeds, you will become bad. To become the person you want to be, act as if you already are that kind of person. Each of us chooses what kind of person we will become. To become a good person, do the things a good person does. To become a bad person, do the things a bad person does. The opportunity to take action to become the kind of person you want to be is yours.

Educate Yourself
Read Like A Wolf Eats
Be Excellent to Each Other
Books Then, Books Now, Books Forever

***

In this retelling, as in all my retellings, I have tried to make the work of literature accessible to modern readers who may lack some of the knowledge about mythology, religion, and history that the literary work's contemporary audience had.

Do you know a language other than English? If you do, I give you permission to translate this book, copyright your translation, publish or self-publish it, and keep all the royalties for yourself. (Do give me credit, of course, for the original retelling.)

I would like to see my retellings of classic literature used in schools, so I give permission to the country of Finland (and all other countries) to give copies of this book to all students forever. I also give permission to the state of Texas (and all other states) to give copies of this book to all students forever. I also give permission to all teachers to give copies of this book to all students forever.

Teachers need not actually teach my retellings. Teachers are welcome to give students copies of my eBooks as background material. For example, if they are teaching Homer's *Iliad* and *Odyssey*, teachers are welcome to give students copies of my *Virgil's* Aeneid: *A Retelling in Prose* and tell students, "Here's another ancient epic you may want to read in your spare time."

CAST OF CHARACTERS

MALE CHARACTERS

FERDINAND, King of Navarre. King Ferdinand falls in love with the Princess of France.

BIRON, Lord, attending on the King. Biron falls in love with Rosaline.

LONGAVILLE, Lord, attending on the King. Longaville falls in love with Maria.

DUMAIN, Lord, attending on the King. Dumain falls in love with Katherine.

BOYET, MARCADÉ, Lords, attending on the Princess of France.

DON ADRIANO DE ARMADO, a fantastical Spaniard.

SIR NATHANIEL, a Curate.

HOLOFERNES, a Schoolmaster.

DULL, a Constable.

COSTARD, a Clown.

MOTE, Page to Armado.

A Forester.

FEMALE CHARACTERS

The PRINCESS of France.

ROSALINE, MARIA, KATHERINE, Ladies, attending on the Princess. Rosaline is a black woman.

JAQUENETTA, a country Wench.

MINOR CHARACTERS

Officers and Others, Attendants on the King and the Princess.

SCENE: Navarre.

NOTES:

For the translations of the Latin quotations in Act 4, scene 2, I used the Folger Shakespeare Library edition of *Love's Labor's Lost*:

Shakespeare, William. *Love's Labor's Lost*. Ed. Barbara A. Mowat and Paul Werstine. New York. Simon & Schuster Paperbacks, 1996. Print.

In this society, the word "wench" was not necessarily negative. It was often used affectionately.

CHAPTER 1

— 1.1 —

In his park — an expanse of land stocked with game birds and animals — Ferdinand, the King of Navarre, was talking with his attendants Biron, Longaville, and Dumain. Navarre was a small country in between France and Spain. Attendants can be nobles, as is the case with Biron, Longaville, and Dumain. As he talked, King Ferdinand held a document.

King Ferdinand said, "Let fame, which all men hunt after in their lives, live inscribed upon the bronze plates of our tombs and then grace — honor — us in the disgrace of death, when, in spite of cormorant-devouring Time, the endeavor of this present breath and life may buy that honor which shall dull the keen edge of Death's scythe and make us heirs of all eternity."

Death can be disgraceful because it results in the rotting of our bodies, but one way that we can disgrace death is by achieving fame and having our reputation continue to live after our bodies die.

The time that we have to live is short because Time is like the greedy bird named the cormorant. The cormorant gulps its prey, and Time gulps the minutes and hours and more of our lives.

King Ferdinand continued, "Therefore, brave conquerors — for so you are, you who war against your own affections and passions and the huge army of the world's desires. Our recent edict shall strongly stand in force: Navarre shall be the wonder of the world because our court shall be a little Academy, calm and contemplative in the art of proper living.

"You three, Biron, Longaville, and Dumain, have sworn to live with me as my fellow-scholars for a term of three years, and to keep those statutes that are recorded in this document here. Your oaths are spoken, and now you must sign your names, so that the evidence of his own handwriting may strike down the honor of the man who violates the smallest clause written here in this document.

"If you are armed — properly prepared — to do as you have sworn to do, sign your name to your deep and solemn oaths, and keep your oaths, too."

Longaville said, "I am resolved to keep my oath. It is only a fast lasting three years. The mind shall banquet, though the body pine and starve. Fat paunches have lean pates — heads and what is in them — and dainty bits make the ribs fat, but quite bankrupt the wits."

Longaville signed the document.

Dumain said, "My loving lord, I — Dumain — am mortified: I am dead to Earthly pleasures. The grosser and cruder kind of these delights of the world I — Dumain — throw upon the gross world's baser slaves. Let lesser people enjoy such lesser pleasures.

"When it comes to love, wealth, and pomp, I pine and die — I reject them all. Instead of enjoying such pleasures, with all these others who sign the oath I will live a philosophic life."

Dumain signed the document.

Biron said, "I can only repeat what Longaville and Dumain have already said. So much, dear liege, I have already sworn. That is, I have already sworn to live and study here three years.

"But there are other strict observances such as not to see a woman in that term of three years, which I very much hope is not written there. And other strict observances such as one day in a week to touch no food and to eat only one meal on each of the other six days, which I hope is not written there. And then such other strict observances as to sleep only three hours in the night, and not be seen to shut one's eyes during all the day, which I fervently hope is not written there — I have been accustomed to think no harm all night and to make a dark night also of half the day."

Biron was thinking of this proverb: He who drinks well sleeps well, and he who sleeps well thinks no harm. He was accustomed to sleeping all night and napping much of the day.

Biron continued, "Oh, these are barren tasks, too hard to keep — to not see ladies, to study, to fast, and to not sleep!"

King Ferdinand said, "Your oath is passed to pass away from these. You swore an oath to renounce all of these."

"Let me say no, my liege, if you please," Biron replied. "I swore only to study with your grace and to stay here in your court for the space of three years."

Longaville said, "You swore to that, Biron, and to all the rest."

"By yea and nay, sir, then I swore in jest," Biron said.

Matthew 5:37 of the King James Bible states, *"But let your communication be, Yea, yea; Nay, nay: for whatsoever is more than these cometh of evil."*

Matthew 5:37 says to swear either yes or no, but Biron was saying that he had sworn both yes and no — yes to part of the oath, and no to the rest of the oath. When he had sworn to the oath, he was agreeing to keep part of the oath, but the rest of his swearing was only in jest.

Biron then asked, "What is the end — the purpose — of study? Let me know."

King Ferdinand replied, "Why, to know that which otherwise we would not know."

"So you mean things hidden and barred from common sense?" Biron asked.

"Yes, that is study's godlike recompense," King Ferdinand said.

"Come on, then; I will swear to study so that I will know the thing I am forbidden to know," Biron said. "For example, I will study where I may dine well, when to feast I expressly am forbidden. Or I will study where to meet some fine mistress, when mistresses from common sense are hidden. Or, having sworn to a too-hard-to-keep oath, I will study how to break it and yet not break my word — my troth."

A "mistress" can be a woman who is respected and loved. A "mistress" is not necessarily a sexual partner.

Biron continued, "If study's gain be thus and this be so, study knows that which yet it does not know. Ask me to swear an oath to learn this, and I will never say no. This is the kind of hidden and secret knowledge that I would like to know."

King Ferdinand said, "These things you talk about are the stops — the obstructions — that hinder study quite and tempt our intellects to indulge in vain delight."

Biron said, "Why, all delights are vain, but the delight is most vain that with pain purchased does acquire pain — the most vain delight is one that is acquired with difficulty and also brings difficulty with it."

Pursuing such a delight is done in vain. An archaic meaning of the word "vain" is "foolish," and so pursuing such a delight is foolish. Why pursue something that will bring you pain when that pain is not worth the price to acquire it?

Biron continued, "For example, painfully to pore upon a book to seek the light of truth, while truth the while does treacherously blind the eyesight of its look — its sight. Light seeking light does light of light beguile and cheat. So, before you find where light in darkness lies — before you discover the clarification of obscure and esoteric knowledge — your light grows dark by the loss of your eyesight."

Biron was referring to the belief that engaging in excessive reading could make one blind.

Biron continued, "Let me study how to please the eye indeed by fixing it upon a fairer eye — the eye of a woman. Such a fairer eye will dazzle the beholder, and although it will blind him, it yet shall be his guiding light and give him the light that blinded him.

"Study is like the Heaven's glorious Sun that will not be deeply searched with saucy and insolent looks. The Sun will not permit you at stare at it.

"Little have continual plodders ever won except base authority from others' books.

"The original astronomers named the planets. These Earthly godfathers of Heaven's lights — the astronomers — who give Biron was equivocating. Becoming a great scholar can get one a name — a reputation — but that is a different kind of name from the name that a godfather can bestow.

to every planet get no more profit from their shining, starlit nights than those who walk and don't know what the names of the planets are."

Astronomers are learned people who give names to planets the way that godfathers give names to infants, but how much practical and personal profit can a person get out of naming — or knowing the names of — the planets? We can learn about constellations and such things by reading books, but is that knowledge practical?

Biron continued, "To know too much is to know nothing but fame, and every godfather can give a name."

"Fame" is "what is said about something." The excessive studying of books results in a lack of knowledge through personal experience: One knows little more than what one has read. True, an acquisition of knowledge by the excessive studying of books can get one a name — but a name is something that any godfather can bestow.

King Ferdinand said, "How well Biron has read! He is able to reason against reading!"

Dumain said, "He has proceeded — argued — well in his attempt to stop all good proceeding — all good advancement of knowledge!"

One meaning of "to proceed" is "to get a university degree." Dumain was saying in part that Biron was proceeding to make arguments in order to keep others from proceeding — from getting a university degree.

Longaville said, "He weeds the wheat and still lets grow the weeding."

He meant that Biron was pulling up the wheat and allowing the weeds to grow. Biron was praising the wrong thing and dispraising the right thing.

Biron replied, "The spring is near when green geese are a-breeding."

Green geese are young geese that cackle. Here Biron was saying that Dumain and Longaville were cackling — making critical comments about him — as if they were green geese — young fools.

Dumain asked, "How does what you said follow from what we said?"

"It is fit, aka suitable, in its place and time," Biron replied.

"In reason what you said is nothing," Dumain said. "It makes no sense."

Biron made a reference to "no rhyme or reason" by saying, "It is something then in rhyme." If something is with no rhyme or reason, it has no reasonable explanation or purpose.

Maybe Dumain did not understand the reason why Biron had said what he said, but he could understand that "weeding" and "a-breeding" rhymed.

King Ferdinand said, "Biron is like a malicious sneaping and nipping frost that bites the first-born infants — the buds — of the spring."

"Well, let's say I am," Biron said. "Why should proud summer boast before the birds have any cause to sing? Why should I take joy in any abortive — stopping before it starts — birth? At Christmas I no more desire a rose than I wish for a snow during May's new-fangled mirth. Instead, I like each thing that in season grows."

Earlier, Biron had argued against excessive studying. Now, he was arguing against doing things out of season. Things ought to be done at the right time for doing them. Each natural season has its own delights; each time of a man's life has its own delights. Yes, there is a time for intensive study, but Biron and the others were past that time — they were too old to be pupils. Now was the time for them to pursue ladies.

Biron added, "So I say to you that to study now is too late. It would be like climbing over the house to unlock the little gate."

"To climb over the house to unlock the little gate" is "to do something absurd."

King Ferdinand said, "Well, you should sit this oath out. Go home, Biron. Adieu."

"No, my good lord," Biron said. "I have sworn to stay with you, and although you can say I have spoken more in favor of barbarism and uncivilized ignorance than for that angel knowledge you have spoken in favor of, yet, confident, I'll keep what I have sworn and endure the penance of each day of each of the three years.

"Give me the paper; let me read the same, and to the strictest decrees I'll sign my name."

King Ferdinand handed the document to Biron and said, "How well this yielding rescues you from shame!"

Biron read out loud, "*Item: That no woman shall come within a mile of my court.*"

He asked, "Has this item been publicly proclaimed?"

Longaville replied, "Yes, four days ago."

Biron said, "Let me read the penalty.

He read out loud, "*On pain of losing her tongue.*"

He asked, "Who devised this penalty?"

"Indeed, that did I," Longaville said.

"Sweet lord, why?" Biron asked.

"To frighten them away from here with that dread penalty," Longaville replied.

"It is a dangerous law against gentility, good manners, and civilized behavior!" Biron said.

He read out loud, "*Item: If any man be seen to talk with a woman within the term of three years, he shall endure such public shame as the rest of the court can possibly devise.*"

Biron said to King Ferdinand, "This article, my liege, you yourself must break, for you know well that the French King's daughter, who is a maiden of grace and complete majesty, is coming here as an ambassador to speak with yourself about surrendering the territory of Aquitaine to her decrepit, sick, and bedridden father. Therefore, this article was made in vain, or else the admired Princess comes vainly hither."

"What do you say, lords?" King Ferdinand said. "Why, this was quite forgotten."

"Excessive study evermore — always — overshoots and misses the target," Biron said. "While excessive study does study to have what it would, it forgets to do the thing that it should, and when it has the thing it hunts for most, it is won as towns are with fire — so won, so lost."

In times of warfare, an enemy town can be set on fire so that it can be won. Setting the town on fire can win — conquer — the town, but often the town is also lost — destroyed — because of the fire.

A person committed to study may learn and so get what he would — what he wants — but that person may lose what he should be getting; for example, he may lose out on getting a wife.

King Ferdinand said, "We must because of necessity dispense with and set aside this decree. The French Princess must necessarily reside here in the palace."

Biron said, "Necessity will make us all break our oaths three thousand times within this three years' space. Every man is born with his own passions, and these passions are not mastered by his efforts and might — mastering these passions requires the special grace of God.

"If I break my oath, this phrase shall speak for me; I am forsworn on 'complete necessity.' And so to the items of the oath at large I write my name."

He signed his name on the document.

Biron added, "And he who breaks any of these items in the least degree stands in attainder of — condemned to — eternal shame. Temptations are to other men as to me. But I believe, although I seem so loath to sign my name, I am the last who will last keep his oath."

Biron's words were ambiguous. He may have meant that he was the last man to sign his name to the oath and he was the last man who would keep the oath — in other words, he would not keep his oath. Or he may have meant that he was the last man to sign his name to the oath and he was the man who would longest keep the oath.

He then asked, "But is there no quick and lively recreation allowed to us?"

"Yes, there is," King Ferdinand replied. "Our court, you know, is frequently visited by a refined traveller from Spain. He is a man rooted in all the world's new fashions, and he has a mint of phrases in his brain. He is one whom the music of his own vain tongue ravishes like enchanting harmony. He is a man of compliments, courteous manners, and nice distinctions, whom right and wrong have chosen to act as umpire of their state of discord. This child of fancy, this fantastic creature, who is Armado hight [named], during the intermissions of our studies shall relate in high-born words the worth of many a knight from tawny, sun-burnt Spain lost in the world's debate — he will tell us about many knights who died in the world's wars. Such stories are told in Spanish chivalric romances.

"What you delight in, my lords, I don't know, not I. But, I protest, I love to hear him lie, and I will use him for my entertainment."

Biron said, "Armado is a most illustrious wight, a man of fire-new, fresh-from-the-mint words, and he is fashion's own knight."

Armado used affected language, and so King Ferdinand and Biron were using affected words as they talked about him. "Hight" means "named," and "wight" means "man."

"Costard the swain and Armado shall be our entertainment," Longaville said. "And so let's begin to study; three years is only a short time."

A "swain" is a "rural fellow" or a "yokel." The word "costard" meant both "a large apple" and "a head."

Anthony Dull and Costard walked over to King Ferdinand, Biron, Longaville, and Dumain. Dull, a constable, was carrying a letter.

Dull asked, "Which is the Duke's own person?"

By "Duke," he meant King Ferdinand. In this society, "Duke" meant "Ruler," and so it was synonymous with "King."

"This man, fellow," Biron replied. "What do you want?"

"I myself reprehend his own person, for I am his grace's tharborough," Dull said, "but I would see his own person in flesh and blood."

Dull made malapropisms. Instead of the word "reprehend," he meant "represent." The word "reprehend" means "reprimand." By "tharborough," Dull meant "farborough," a kind of constable.

"This is he," Biron said, indicating King Ferdinand.

"Signior Arme ... Arme ... commends you," Dull said. He could not pronounce "Armado." He also should have said, "commends himself to you," not "commends you."

Constable Dull handed King Ferdinand the letter and added, "There's villainy abroad. This letter will tell you more."

"Sir, the contempts thereof the letter are as touching — concerning — me," Costard said.

Costard meant "contents," not "contempts," although "contempts" was a fitting word for the contents of the letter.

Reading the letter, King Ferdinand said, "This is a letter from the magnificent Armado."

"However low is the matter — the content — of the letter, I hope in God for high words," Biron said.

He was hoping that the letter used highfalutin language even if the content of the letter was trivial. Such a letter would be funny. Biron was well aware of Armado's penchant for fancy words.

"That is a high hope for a low Heaven — a high hope for a small blessing," Longaville said. "That's not much to hope highly for. May God grant us patience!"

"Patience to hear?" Biron asked. "Or patience to refrain from laughing?"

"To hear meekly, sir, and to laugh moderately," Longaville said. "Or to refrain from both."

"Well, sir, it may be that the style shall give us cause to climb in the merriness," Biron said.

He was punning on "style" and "stile" — a stile consisted of steps that allowed people to climb over a wall or a fence.

Costard said, "The matter is to me, sir, as concerning Jaquenetta. The manner of it — the state of the case — is, I was taken with the manner — I was caught in the act."

"In what manner?" Biron asked.

Costard replied, "In manner and form following, sir."

This was a legal formula used to introduce a detailed description of a crime.

Costard continued, "All these three — manner, form, and following — as I will describe now.

"I was seen with her in the manor-house, sitting with her upon the form — the bench — and taken following her into the park, which, put together, is 'in manner and form following.' Now, sir, as for the manner — it is the manner of a man to speak to a woman. As for the form — in some form."

Costard had followed Jaquenetta, a rural woman, because he wanted to talk to her. The manner of a man is to want to talk to a woman. The word "manner" means "the way things are done." As for the form, a woman has a womanly form.

Biron asked, "Is the form the reason for the following, sir?"

Costard replied, "As it shall follow in my correction — my punishment — and may God defend the right!"

The words "May God defend the right" were used in trials by combat. A high-ranking person could accuse another high-ranking person of a capital crime. If no proof were available, the two could fight to the death. The reasoning was that God would ensure that the person who was in the right would kill the person who was in the wrong. Whoever lost the combat, therefore, was guilty.

King Ferdinand asked Biron, Longaville, and Dumain, "Will you listen carefully and attentively to this letter?"

Biron answered, "We will, just as if we were listening to the words of an oracle."

An oracle of the gods answers important questions.

Costard, who knew the contents of the letter, said, "Such is the sinplicity of man to hearken after the flesh."

Some of his malapropisms were appropriate: "sinplicity," in place of "simplicity."

King Ferdinand read out loud, "*Great deputy, the welkin's vicegerent and sole dominator of Navarre, my soul's earth's god, and my body's fostering patron.*"

King Ferdinand was "the welkin's vicegerent." He was a ruler on Earth, and as such he was God's deputy on Earth. This culture believed that God chose who would be King.

Costard said, "Not a word of Costard yet."

King Ferdinand read out loud, "*So it is —*"

"It may be so, but if he says it is so, he is, when it comes to telling the truth, only so-so," Costard said.

King Ferdinand ordered, "Peace!"

Costard replied, "May peace belong to me and to every man who dares not fight!"

King Ferdinand said, "By 'Peace,' I mean, 'Be quiet.' Say no more words."

"Say no more words of other men's secrets, I beg you," Costard said.

King Ferdinand read out loud, "*So it is, besieged with sable-colored melancholy, I did commend the black-oppressing humor to the most wholesome physic of thy health-giving air; and, as I am a gentleman, betook myself to walk. The time when? About the sixth hour; when beasts most graze, birds best peck, and men sit down to that nourishment which is called supper: so much for the time when. Now for the ground which; which, I mean, I walked upon: it is yclept thy park.*"

Armado used all those words to say this: I was feeling depressed, and so, around suppertime, I took a walk in your park.

King Ferdinand read out loud, "*Then for the place where; where, I mean, I did encounter that obscene and preposterous event, that draweth from my snow-white pen the ebony-colored ink, which here thou viewest, beholdest, surveyest, or seest; but to the place where; it standeth north-north-east and by east from the west corner of thy curious-knotted garden: there did I see that low-spirited swain, that base minnow of thy mirth*" —

Armado used all those words to say this: There in the park near your garden I saw something I consider obscene that caused me to write you this letter.

He compared the perpetrator of the something obscene to a minnow — a small, insignificant fish. He saw the something obscene near the curious-knotted garden — fashionable decorative gardens of the time were laid out in intricate designs.

Costard asked, "Me?"

King Ferdinand read out loud, "*that unlettered small-knowing soul*" —

The word "unlettered" means "uneducated."

Costard asked, "Me?"

King Ferdinand read out loud, "*that shallow vassal*" —

Costard asked, "Still me?"

King Ferdinand read out loud, "*who, as I remember, hight Costard*" —

Costard said, "Oh, it is me!"

King Ferdinand read out loud, "*who, sorted and consorted, contrary to thy established proclaimed edict and continent canon, which with — oh, with — but with this I passion to say wherewith*" —

Armado used the word "passion" as a verb meaning "grieve." "Sorted and consorted" meant "associated and accompanied."

Costard said, "He is going to write that he found me with a wench."

The word "wench" meant "woman" and was often used affectionately.

King Ferdinand read out loud, "*— with a child of our grandmother Eve, a female; or, for thy more sweet understanding, a woman. Him I, as my ever-esteemed duty pricks me on, have sent to thee, to receive the meed of punishment, by thy sweet grace's officer, Anthony Dull; a man of good repute, carriage, bearing, and estimation.*"

Dull said, "That is me, if it shall please you; I am Anthony Dull."

King Ferdinand read out loud, "*For Jaquenetta — so is the weaker vessel called whom I apprehended with the aforesaid swain — I keep her as a vessel of the law's fury; and I shall, at the least of thy sweet notice, bring her to trial. Thine, in all compliments of devoted and heart-burning heat of duty.*"

Armado had used all those words to say this: I have arrested Jaquenetta and as soon as you, King Ferdinand, give the order, I will put her on trial.

The letter was signed, "DON ADRIANO DE ARMADO."

Biron said, "This is not so well as I looked for, but the best that ever I heard."

King Ferdinand said, "Yes, the best for the worst — this is an excellent example of a badly written and pretentious letter."

He then asked Costard, "But, sirrah, what do you say about this?"

"Sirrah" was a word used to address a man of much lower social rank than the speaker.

"Sir, I confess to being with the wench," Costard replied.

"Did you hear the proclamation about not being in the company of women?" King Ferdinand asked.

"I do confess much of the hearing it, but little of the marking of it," Costard said. "I heard it, but I did not pay much attention to it."

"It was proclaimed that a man would be imprisoned for a year if he were caught with a wench," King Ferdinand said.

"I was not taken with a wench, sir. I was taken with a damsel."

"Well, the proclamation also used the word 'damsel.'"

"She was no damsel, sir. She was a virgin."

"The proclamation used many different words for a woman, including the word 'virgin.'"

"If the proclamation did use the word 'virgin,' then I deny her virginity. I was taken with a maiden."

"This maiden will not serve your turn, sir," King Ferdinand replied.

He meant that using the word "maiden" would not keep Costard from being punished.

"This maiden will serve my turn, sir," Costard said.

He meant that the maiden would serve him sexually.

King Ferdinand said, "Sir, I will pronounce your sentence: You shall fast for a week with bran and water."

Costard said, "I had rather pray a month with mutton soup."

In this society, the word "mutton" was sometimes used to refer to a whore.

King Ferdinand continued, "And Don Armado shall be your jail keeper.

"My Lord Biron, see that Costard is delivered over to Don Armado.

"And now we go, lords, to put in practice that which each to the others has so strongly sworn. It is time that we begin to study."

King Ferdinand, Longaville, and Dumain exited.

Biron said, "I'll bet my head against any goodman's hat that these oaths and laws will prove to be an idle scorn. They are useless and ought to be scorned."

A goodman is a man with a rank below that of a noble. The title "goodman" especially applies to a farmer or a yeoman, aka freeholder.

Biron then said to Costard, "Sirrah, come on."

"I suffer for the truth, sir," Costard said. "For it is true that I was caught with Jaquenetta, and Jaquenetta is a true girl, and therefore I welcome the sour cup of prosperity! Affliction may one day smile again; and until then, sit thee down and keep me company, sorrow!"

Costard had mixed up his words, using "prosperity" when he meant "affliction," and vice versa.

—1.2—

Don Adriano de Armado was talking to Mote, his young page, in King Ferdinand's park. A page is a youthful attendant to a person of high rank.

Armado said, "Boy, what sign is it when a man of great spirit grows melancholy?"

He expected that Mote would answer that it is a sign that the man of great spirit is in love, but Mote answered, "It is a great sign, sir, that he will look sad."

Armado said, "Why, sadness is one and the self-same thing as melancholy, dear imp."

"No, no," Mote said. "Oh, Lord, sir, no."

"How can thou distinguish between sadness and melancholy, my tender juvenal?"

By "juvenal," Armado meant "juvenile."

Mote replied, "By an easily understandable demonstration of the application, my tough signior."

Mote was punning on "signior" and "senior."

"Why tough signior? Why tough signior?" Armado asked.

"Why tender juvenal? Why tender juvenal?" Mote answered.

"I spoke it, tender juvenal, as a congruent epitheton appertaining to thy young days, which we may nominate 'tender,'" Armado said.

"Congruent epithon" is a fancy way of saying "appropriate description."

Mote said, "And I, tough signior, as an appertinent title to your old age, which we may name 'tough.'"

"Appertinent" is an obsolete, fancy way of saying "appertaining" or "suitable." Mote was mocking Armado's use of fancy words.

Armado commented, "Pretty and apt."

"What do you mean, sir?" Mote asked. "That I am pretty, and my saying is apt? Or that I am apt, and my saying is pretty?"

"Thou art pretty, because thou art little."

"I am little pretty, because I am little," Mote said. "Wherefore am I apt?"

Armado replied, "And therefore you are apt, because you are quick."

"Are you saying that to praise me, master?" Mote asked.

"Yes, I say it in thy condign praise."

"Condign" means "well-deserved."

Mote said, "I will praise an eel with the same praise."

"You will praise an eel by saying that it is quick — ingenious?" Armado asked.

"I will praise an eel by saying that it is quick — swift," Mote said.

"I do say that thou art quick in answers," Armado said. "Thou heatest my blood."

Hot blood is angry blood.

"I understand, sir," Mote said.

"I love not to be crossed," Armado said.

Mote thought, *He speaks the complete opposite of the truth; he loves crosses, but crosses do not love him.*

In this society, coins were decorated with crosses.

"I have promised to study three years with the Duke," Armado said.

"You may do it in an hour, sir," Mote said.

"That is impossible."

"How many is one counted three times — one times three?"

"I am ill at reckoning," Armado said. "I am bad at math; math is something suitable for a tapster, aka bartender — someone who lacks my great spirit."

"You are a gentleman and a gamester, sir," Mote said.

A gamester is a gambler.

"I confess to being both," Armado said. "They are both the varnish — polish — of a complete man."

"Then, I am sure, you know how much the gross sum of deuce-ace amounts to."

A deuce-ace is a throw of the dice resulting in a one and a two.

"It doth amount to one more than two," Armado said.

"And that is what the low-born common people call three," Mote said.

"That is true."

Mote said, "Why, sir, is this such a piece of study? Was that hard? Now here you have completed your study of three, even before you have blinked three times. How easy it is to join the word 'years' to the word 'three,' and then you can study three years in two words, the dancing horse will tell you."

The dancing horse was a famous performing horse of the time named Morocco (or Marocco). In addition to dancing, it would use its hoof to tap out numbers on the ground, seemingly solving simple arithmetic problems.

"That is a most fine figure!" Armado said.

The figure was a figure of speech, or word play. A figure is also a number. Mote thought, *This figure proves that you are a cipher.*

A cipher is a zero — it is nothing.

"I will hereupon confess that I am in love," Armado said, "and as it is base for a soldier to love, so am I in love with a base — low-born — wench. If drawing my sword against the disposition of affection would deliver me from the reprobate thought of it, I would take Desire prisoner, and ransom him to any French courtier for a newly devised courtesy such as a new fashionable bow. I think it would be scornful to sigh. Methinks I should outswear Cupid. Comfort, me, boy, by telling me what great men have been in love."

"Hercules is a great man who has been in love, master," Mote answered.

"Most sweet Hercules!" Armado said. "Give me some more authoritative examples, dear boy. Name some more, and, my sweet child, let them be men of good reputation and carriage."

One meaning of the word "carriage" is "bearing or demeanor." Mote, however, used it in a different sense.

"Samson, master," Mote replied. "He was a man of good carriage, great carriage, for he carried the town-gates on his back like a porter, and he was in love."

Judges 16:3 states this: "*And Samson slept till midnight, and arose at midnight, and took the doors of the gates of the city and the two posts, and lifted them away with the bars, and put them upon his shoulders, and carried them up to the top of the mountain that is before Hebron*" (1599 Geneva Bible).

"Oh, well-knit, strongly built Samson!" Armado said. "Strong-jointed Samson! I do excel thee in my rapier as much as thou didst me in carrying gates. I am in love, too. Who was Samson's love, my dear Mote?"

"A woman, master."

"Of what complexion?"

One meaning of the word "complexion" is "disposition or temperament."

Mote replied, "Of all the four, or the three, or the two, or one of the four."

This society believed that the mixture of four humors in the body determined one's temperament. One humor could be predominant. The four humors are blood, yellow bile, black bile, and phlegm. If blood is predominant, then the person is sanguine (optimistic). If yellow bile is predominant, then the person is choleric (bad-tempered). If black bile is predominant, then the person is melancholic (sad). If phlegm is predominant, then the person is phlegmatic (calm).

Armado said, "Tell me precisely of what complexion."

Instead of understanding "complexion" to mean "disposition or temperament," Mote deliberately misinterpreted it to mean skin coloring.

"Of the sea-water green, sir," Mote said.

Many young girls of the time suffered from "green-sickness." Falling in love was thought to cause this illness, but we now believe that the young girls were actually anemic from iron deficiency.

"Is that one of the four complexions?" Armado asked.

"I have read that, sir; and it is the best of them, too," Mote said.

"Green indeed is the color of lovers; but to have a love of that color, methinks Samson had small reason for it," Armado said. "He surely affected — loved — her for her wit."

One reason green is the color of lovers is that young women would meet their lovers and get what was called a green gown. The women would lie on their backs and get grass stains on their gowns.

"It was so, sir," Mote said, "for she had a green wit."

A green wit is an immature wit, aka immature intelligence.

"My love is most immaculate white and red," Armado said.

"Most maculate thoughts, master, are masked under such colors," Mote said.

The word "immaculate" means "unstained"; "maculate thoughts" are "stained or sinful thoughts."

"Define, define, well-educated infant," Armado said. "Explain what you mean."

"My father's wit and my mother's tongue, assist me!" Mote said, deliberately changing the phrase "mother's wit."

"Sweet invocation of a child," Armado said. "That was very pretty and pathetical! That was very pretty and moving!"

Mote sang this song:
"If she be made of white and red,
"Her faults will never be known,
"For blushing cheeks by faults are bred
"And fears by pale white shown:
"Then if she fear, or be to blame,
"By this you shall not know,
"For still her cheeks possess the same
"Which naturally she does own."

Maculate thoughts are sinful thoughts and thinking them in the company of others can cause a white-skinned person to be embarrassed by having blameworthy thoughts and to blush red, thus allowing other persons to know that the blushing person is embarrassed. And fear causes a Caucasian to grow pale, or white. But if a person has a complexion naturally composed of white blotches and red blotches, then who knows what that person is thinking?

Mote said, "This is a dangerous rhyme, master, against the cause of white and red."

Armado asked, "Is there not a ballad, boy, of the King and the Beggar?"

In this society, ballads about "King Cophetua and the Beggar-Maiden" were common at one time. King Cophetua was an African who had no interest in women until he saw a beggar-maiden named Penelophon and fell in love with her.

Mote replied, "The world was very guilty of such a ballad some three ages ago, but I think now it is not to be found; or, if it were, it would be acceptable neither for the writing nor the tune."

"I will have that subject newly writ over, so that I may example my digression by some mighty precedent," Armado said.

His "digression" was a "moral lapse." He wanted to have a new version of the ballad written because it would show that another man — who was great — was guilty of the same digression or transgression as he.

He added, "Boy, I love that country girl whom I took in the park with the rational hind Costard. She deserves well."

A rational hind is a yokel who is capable of showing some intelligence.

By "took," Armado meant "arrested."

Mote thought, *She well deserves to be whipped; and yet she deserves a better lover than my master.*

In this society, law officials punished prostitutes by whipping them.

"Sing, boy," Armado said. "My spirit grows heavy in love."

"And that's a great marvel because you love a light wench," Mote said.

Light wenches were promiscuous women who had light heels that could be easily lifted in the air along with parted knees.

"I say, sing," Armado said.

"Wait until this company of people has passed by," Mote said.

Constable Dull, Costard, and Jaquenetta walked up to them.

Dull said to Armado, "Sir, the Duke's pleasure is that you keep Costard secure, and you must suffer him to take no delight nor no penance, but he must fast three days a week."

Instead of "penance," Dull meant to say "pleasance," which means "pleasure."

Dull continued, "As for this damsel, I must keep her at the park. She has been assigned the job of being a dairy-maiden. Fare you well."

"I betray myself with blushing," Armado said.

He was thinking sinful thoughts.

He said to Jaquenetta, "Maiden!"

She replied, "Man."

"I will visit thee at the lodge."

"That's nearby."

"I know where it is situated."

"Lord, how wise you are!"

"I will tell thee wonders," Armado said.

"With that face?" Jaquenetta replied.

This was an idiomatic expression that meant, "Really? I don't believe you!"

"I love thee," Armado said.

"So I heard you say," Jaquenetta replied.

This was another idiomatic expression that meant, "Really? I don't believe you!"

"And so, farewell."

"May fair weather follow you!" Jaquenetta said.

Constable Dull said, "Come, Jaquenetta, let's go!"

Dull and Jaquenetta exited.

Armado said to Costard, "Villain, thou shalt fast for thy offences before thou shalt be pardoned."

"Well, sir, I hope, when I do it, I shall do it on a full stomach," Costard said.

"On a full stomach" was an idiomatic expression meaning "courageously."

Armado said, "Thou shalt be heavily punished."

"I am more bound to you than your servants are bound to you, for they are but lightly rewarded," Costard said.

Armado said to Mote, "Take away this villain; shut him up."

Mote said to Costard, "Come, you transgressing slave; let's go!"

Costard said to Armado, "Let me not be pent up, sir. I will fast, being loose."

He meant that he would fast even if he were loose and not shut up in a cell, but his words could also be interpreted as saying that he would fast as a treatment for having loose bowels.

"No, sir," Mote said. "That would be fast and loose."

"Fast and loose" was the name of a rope trick that con men pulled to make money.

Mote added, "You shall go to prison."

"Well, if ever I do see the merry days of desolation that I have seen, some shall see."

Costard meant to say "jubilation," not "desolation."

Mote asked, "What shall some see?"

"Nothing, Master Mote, but what they look upon," Costard said. "It is not for prisoners to be too silent in their words, and therefore I will say nothing. I thank God I have as little patience as another man; and therefore I can be quiet."

As usual, Costard misused words. Instead of "silent," he meant to say "loud." And he had meant to say "as much patience," not "as little patience."

Mote and Costard exited, leaving Armado alone.

Armado said to himself, "I do affect the very ground, which is base, where her shoe, which is baser, guided by her foot, which is basest, doth tread."

By "affect," he meant "love." Even when talking to himself, he used and misused both fancy words and ordinary words. Or perhaps he really meant that Jaquenetta's foot was baser — nastier — than her shoe.

He continued, "I shall be forsworn, which is a great argument — evidence — of falsehood, if I love."

Yes, perjury — falsely swearing — is great evidence of falsehood.

He continued, "And how can that be true love which is falsely attempted? Love is a familiar, a spirit attending a witch; Love is a devil — there is no evil angel but Love.

"Yet was Samson so tempted, and he had an excellent strength; yet was Solomon so seduced, and he had a very good wit. Cupid's butt-shaft — blunt arrow — is too hard for Hercules' club; and therefore too much odds for this Spaniard's rapier.

"The first and second cause will not serve my turn."

Armado was thinking about having a duel with Cupid, the god who shot arrows that caused people to fall in love. The first and second causes of fighting a duel were being accused of committing a capital crime such as treason, and being accused of being dishonorable. Cupid was causing Armado to commit a crime in violation of King Ferdinand's recently announced law, and he was causing Armado to lose honor by breaking an oath that he had sworn.

He continued, "The *passado* — forward thrust of the rapier — Cupid respects not, and the *duello* — dueling code — Cupid regards not. Cupid's disgrace is to be called 'boy,' but his glory is to subdue men. Adieu, valor! Rust, rapier! Be still, drum! For your manager — master — is in love; yea, he loveth. Assist me, some extemporal god of rhyme, for I am sure I shall turn sonneteer. Devise, wit; write, pen — I am for whole volumes in folio."

Now that Armado was in love, he was going to follow the courtly custom of writing love sonnets to the woman he loved. He was calling upon some god to help him write enough sonnets to fill up a large book — a folio.

CHAPTER 2

— 2.1 —

The Princess of France had arrived in the park of King Ferdinand. With her were her lady attendants Rosaline, Maria, and Katherine, and her male attendant Boyet. Also present were lords and other attendants.

Boyet said, "Now, madam, summon up your dearest spirits, your best powers. Consider whom the King your father sends, to whom he sends, and what's his message. The King your father sends yourself, who is held precious in the world's esteem, to parley with the sole inheritor — possessor — of all perfections that a man may own, the matchless King Ferdinand of Navarre; the issue to be discussed is of no less weight than the territory of Aquitaine, which is valuable enough to be a dowry for a Queen.

"Be now as prodigal of all dear — valuable — grace as Nature was in making graces dear — expensive — when she starved the general world other than yourself and prodigally gave them all to you."

The Princess of France replied, "Good Lord Boyet, my beauty, although it is only average, does not need the painted flourish of your praise. Beauty is bought by the judgment of the eye, not made available by the base sale of merchants' tongues — the flattering praise of merchants trying to sell stuff by calling it beautiful is worthless. I am less proud to hear you count — spell out — my worth than you are much willing to be accounted wise because you spend your wit in the flattering praise of mine.

"But now to task the tasker: You have been tasking me with your false flattery of my 'beauty,' and now I have a task for you. Good Boyet, you are not ignorant that all-telling rumor has noised abroad that the King of Navarre has made a vow that until painstaking and diligent study has worn away three years, no woman may approach his silent court."

Using the royal plural, she said, "Therefore to us it seems a necessary course of action, before we enter his forbidden gates, to know what he wants us to do, and in that behalf and for that purpose, confident of your worthiness, we single you out as our best-moving and most persuasive fair solicitor.

"Tell him that the daughter of the King of France, on serious business, craving quick dispatch of that business, importunes personal conversation with his grace.

"Go quickly to him and say all this, while we wait, like humble-faced petitioners, to learn what his high will desires."

Boyet replied, "Proud to be entrusted with this employment, willingly I go."

"All pride is willing pride, and yours is so," the Princess of France replied. "All pride, including yours, originates in the will — the wish or desire."

Boyet exited to carry out his errand.

The Princess of France asked, "Who are the votaries, my loving lords, who are vow-fellows with this virtuous Duke?"

Votaries are people who have taken an oath or vow.

The first lord said, "Lord Longaville is one."

The Princess asked, "Do you know the man?"

Maria said, "I know him, madam. At a feast celebrating the marriage between Lord Perigort and the beauteous heir of Jaques Falconbridge, which was solemnized in Normandy, I saw this Longaville. He is reputed to be a man of excellent personal qualities. He is interested in culture and arts, and he has a glorious reputation in military matters. He has both a contemplative and an active life. Everything that he puts his mind to becomes him — he does nothing ill that he wants to do well.

"The only soil of his fair virtue's gloss, if virtue's gloss will stain with any soil, is that his sharp wit is matched with too blunt a will. The edge of his wit has the power to cut, and his will always wills — wants — to spare none who come within his power."

The Princess said, "He is probably some merry mocking lord, isn't he?"

"So people say who most know his moods and disposition," Maria said.

"Such short-lived wits do wither as they grow," the Princess said, alluding to the proverb "Soon ripe; soon rotten."

She then asked, "Who are the rest of the votaries?"

Katherine said, "Another is the young Dumain, a well-accomplished youth, one of all whom virtue loves because they love virtue. He has the most power to do most harm, although he least knows evil, because he has the intelligence to make an ill bodily shape seem to be good, and he has a bodily shape that would win grace and favor even if he had no intelligence. I saw him at the

Duke Alencon's once; and my report of his goodness falls very short of his great worthiness."

Rosaline said, "Another of these students was at that time there with Dumain, if I have heard the truth. Biron they call him, and some people called him by the nickname Berowne, which sounds like a sad name — Brown. But a merrier man, within the limit of becoming and suitable mirth, I never spent an hour's talking with. His eye begets occasion for his wit; for every object that his eye catches, his wit turns to a mirth-moving jest, which his fair tongue — the expresser of his fancy — delivers in such apt and gracious words that aged ears play truant and avoid listening to serious discussions in order to listen to his tales and his younger hearers are quite ravished with delight, so sweet and voluble is his discourse."

"God bless my ladies!" the Princess said. "Are they all in love, causing each to garnish her beloved with such adorning ornaments of praise?"

The first lord said, "Here comes Boyet."

Boyet walked over to the group.

The Princess asked, "Now, what admittance shall we enjoy, lord? Shall we be admitted into the palace?"

"The King of Navarre had notice of your fair approach," Boyet replied, "and he and his associates in their oath were all ready to meet you, gentle lady, before I came. Indeed, thus much I have learned. He means to lodge you outdoors, in this field, like one who comes here to besiege his court in wartime, rather than to seek a dispensation for his oath, a dispensation that would let you enter his house, which now lacks servants."

King Ferdinand needed fewer servants because of his avowed dedication to study.

Boyet looked up and said, "Here comes the King of Navarre."

King Ferdinand, Biron, Longaville, Dumain, and some attendants walked over to the group.

King Ferdinand said, "Fair Princess, welcome to the court of Navarre."

The Princess replied, "The word 'fair' I give you back again, and 'welcome' I have not yet had. The roof of this court — the sky — is too high to be yours; and a welcome to the wide fields is too base to be mine."

"You shall be welcome, madam, to my court," King Ferdinand said.

"I will be welcome, then," the Princess said. "Conduct me there."

"Hear me, dear lady," King Ferdinand said. "I have sworn an oath."

"May our Lady help my lord!" the Princess said. "He'll be forsworn and break his oath."

Our Lady is Mary, the mother of Jesus.

"Not for the world, fair madam, by my will," King Ferdinand said.

"By my will" was an oath: "I swear."

"Why, will shall break it," the Princess said. "Will and nothing else."

In her reply, the Princess used "will" to mean both "willpower" and "desire." King Ferdinand's willpower would cause him to break the oath because he desired to break it; in other words, he could break his oath if he chose to, and desire would make him want to and so he would choose to break his oath.

"Your ladyship is ignorant about what my oath is," King Ferdinand said.

The Princess said, "If my lord were ignorant about the content of his oath, his ignorance would be wise, whereas now his knowledge is evidence of his ignorance.

"I hear that your grace has sworn not to be hospitable. It is a deadly sin to keep that oath, my lord, and it is a sin to break it.

"But pardon me. I am too sudden-bold, too hastily presumptuous. To teach an academic — and you are one because you have chosen to pursue knowledge for three years — ill becomes me.

"Please read the purpose of my coming here, and quickly give me a response concerning my petition to you."

"Madam, I will, if quickly I may," King Ferdinand said.

"You will give me a reply all the sooner, so that I can go away," the Princess said, "for you'll prove perjured if you make me stay."

The Princess handed King Ferdinand a document that the King began reading.

Biron asked Rosaline, "Didn't I dance with you in Brabant once?"

Rosaline asked Biron, "Didn't I dance with you in Brabant once?"

"I know you did," Biron said.

"How needless it was then to ask me that question!" Rosaline said.

"You must not be so quick," Biron said, using the word "quick" to mean "impatient, hot-tempered, and sharp and caustic."

Rosaline, deliberately misinterpreting the word "quick" to mean "fast," replied, "My quickness is due to you who spurs me with such questions."

She was alluding to the proverb "Do not spur a willing horse."

Biron said, "Your wit's too hot, it speeds too fast, it will tire."

He was alluding to the proverb "A free horse will soon tire." A free horse is one that has been given the reins; it can run freely without the rider restraining its speed.

Rosaline replied, "Not until it leaves the rider in the mire."

She had no intention of reining in — restraining — her wit.

In an attempt to change the subject, Biron asked, "What time of day is it?"

Rosaline replied, "The hour that fools should ask about."

"Now may fair — good luck — befall your mask!" Biron said.

Like the other noble ladies of the time, Rosaline sometimes wore a mask to protect her face from the Sun when she was outside and she sometimes attended masquerades, but she was not currently wearing a mask.

Rosaline said, "May fair befall the face it covers! May the face under the mask be beautiful!"

"And may your beautiful face send you many loving admirers!" Biron said.

"Amen, as long as you make up none of my many loving admirers!" Rosaline said.

"No, for then I will be gone," Biron said.

Having finished reading the document, and occasionally using the royal plural, King Ferdinand said, "Madam, your father here in this document states that he made the payment of a hundred thousand crowns. That amount is only one half of the entire sum disbursed by my father in the wars waged by your father.

"But let's say that my father or I myself, although neither of us has, received that sum, yet there remains unpaid a hundred thousand more crowns. In security of that loan, one part of the territory of Aquitaine is legally bound to us here in Navarre, although it is not valued as highly as the money that was loaned.

"If then the King your father will restore to us just that one half which is unsettled because it has not been repaid, we will give up our rights in Aquitaine, and we will hold and enjoy fair friendship with his majesty your father.

"But that repayment, it seems, he little intends, because here in this document he demands that we repay the hundred thousand crowns that he claims to have already paid us, and he does not demand, as is his right, on payment to us of a hundred thousand crowns, to have his title to all of Aquitaine restored. He wants us to repay money that we never received, and he wants us to keep our title to part of Aquitaine. We would much rather give up our title to part of Aquitaine and have the money repaid to us that our father lent your father. We prefer to have the money because Aquitaine, as it is, is gelded; it has been divided into two parts and the part we have title to is not worth the amount of money my father lent to your father.

"Dear Princess, were not your father's requests so far from reason's yielding — if they were not so unreasonable — your fair self should make a yielding against some reason in my breast. Your beautiful self would make me generous although right is on my side, and you would go well satisfied to France again."

The Princess replied, "You do the King my father too much wrong, and you wrong the reputation of your name, by seeming not to confess having received that money which has so faithfully been repaid."

"I protest that I never heard of the repayment of that money," King Ferdinand said, "and if you can prove that the money has been repaid, I'll repay it back to the King of France or yield to him Aquitaine."

"We arrest your word," the Princess said. "We seize upon your word as surety that you will do what you just said you will do."

She then said, "Boyet, you can produce acquittances — legal documents showing that the money has been repaid — for such a sum from special officers of Charles, the King of Navarre's father."

"Satisfy me that this is so," King Ferdinand said. "Produce the documents."

Boyet said, "So please your grace, the packet containing those and other legal documents has not yet come. Tomorrow you shall be able to see them."

"That shall be sufficient for me," King Ferdinand said. "At that time I will yield to all reasonable demands. In the meantime, receive such welcome at my hand as honor without breach of honor may make tender of to your true worthiness.

"You may not come, fair Princess, within my gates, but here outside my gates you shall be so received that you shall deem yourself lodged in my heart, although you are denied fair harbor in my house.

"Your own good thoughts will excuse me, and so farewell. Tomorrow we shall visit you again."

The Princess said, "May sweet health and fair desires accompany your grace!"

"Your own wish I wish for you in every aspect!" King Ferdinand said, and then he exited.

Biron said to Rosaline, "Lady, I will commend you to my own heart."

"Please, give my commendations to your heart," Rosaline said. "I would be glad to see it."

"I wish you could hear it groan," Biron said. He was feeling lovesick.

"Is the fool sick?" Rosaline asked.

"Sick at heart."

"Alas, treat your illness by bleeding."

In this society, physicians treated many illnesses by bleeding the patient. Physicians felt that bleeding would help restore the proper proportion of the four humors: blood, yellow bile, black bile, and phlegm. Today, we know that this is quackery.

Biron asked, "Would bleeding my heart do any good?"

"My medical knowledge says that yes, it would."

"Will you prick my heart with your eye?"

In this society, a person in love was thought to shoot a beam out of his or her eyes. The beam would enter the eyes of the loved one and go straight to his or her heart.

Rosaline replied, "*Non point*, but I would with my knife."

"*Non point*" was French for "No point," which has two meanings. Rosaline was saying there was no point to doing as Biron suggested, and her eye had no point and so was incapable of piercing his heart. In contrast, a knife could do that very easily with its point.

"Now, may God save your life!" Biron said.

"And may God save yours from long living!" Rosaline said.

"I cannot stay and give you thanks," Biron said.

He withdrew.

Dumain said to Boyet, "Sir, please, let me have a word with you. What lady is she whom I was talking to?"

"She is the heir of Alencon; Katherine is her name."

"She is a gallant lady. Monsieur, fare you well."

Dumain exited.

Longaville asked Boyet, "Please, let me have a word with you. Who is she in the white dress?"

"She is a woman sometimes, if you saw her in the light."

"Perhaps she is light in the light," Longaville said.

He was punning. Perhaps she would be revealed as a light — promiscuous — woman if seen in the light — if seen properly.

He then said, "I desire her name."

"She has but one for herself; to desire that would be a shame," Boyet replied.

Longaville asked, "Please, sir, whose daughter is she?"

"Her mother's, I have heard."

"God's blessing on your beard!" Longaville said.

He was making the point that Boyet's venerable beard was inconsistent with the joking answers he was making to Longaville's questions. A person capable of growing a beard like that should give serious answers to serious questions.

"Good sir, be not offended," Boyet said. "She is an heir of Falconbridge."

"My anger is ended," Longaville said. "She is a very sweet lady."

"That is not unlikely, sir," Boyet said. "That may be the truth."

Longaville exited.

Biron asked Boyet, "What's the name of the woman wearing the cap?"

"Rosaline, by good hap," Boyet replied. "Rosaline, it so happens."

"Is she wedded or no?"

"She is wedded to her will, sir, or something like that."

One meaning of the word "will" was "sexual desire."

What does "something like that" mean? Biron will find out that Rosaline is single, and so, if Boyet's insinuation is correct, she is a single woman who pursues satisfying her sexual desires.

"You are welcome, sir," Biron said. "Adieu."

Biron's tone was angry because he was not getting a serious answer to his question. Some welcomes are ill. He also did not want to hear that a woman he had fallen in love with was wanton. When he said that Boyet was welcome, he may have been punning: Boyet was well cum — had cum well — as a result of spending time with Rosaline. Personal experience would be one way for Boyet to know that Rosaline was wedded to her will, or something like that.

"Farewell to me, sir, and welcome to you," Boyet replied.

"Welcome to you" meant "You are welcome to go." A proverb of the time stated, "Welcome when you go." Again, some welcomes are ill.

Boyet may have meant this: "I will fare well when you go, and be assured that the next time I welcome you, I will again have well cum."

Some people can say, "Welcome," and make it sound nasty. Boyet was one such person.

Biron exited.

Maria said, "That last man to leave is Biron, the merry madcap lord. You can't speak to him without hearing a jest — not a word with him but a jest."

"And every jest is only a word," Boyet said.

The Princess said, "It was well done of you to take him at his word — you gave him word for word. He likes to engage in argumentative exchanges of words, and you did that."

It is true that Biron liked to engage in wordplay, sometimes malicious, but his questions to Boyet were serious. Boyet, however, was a ladies' man, and he saw in Biron a threat. Here was a case of two men — Biron and Boyet — disliking each other almost at first sight.

"I was as willing to grapple as he was to board," Boyet said.

Boyet was referring to warfare. Two ships would sometimes use grappling hooks to get the ships next to each other so that a ship could be boarded and the sailors fight face to face.

If Biron wanted to board something, that something would be Rosaline's body, but Boyet was willing to grapple with him to keep that from happening, possibly because he wanted to board her — and all the other ladies present.

Note that Rosaline was quiet. Did she not hear Boyet and Biron talking, or was she embarrassed and pretending that she had not heard their conversation?

Maria said, "You were two hot sheeps, indeed."

Biron and Boyet had fought like two angry rams butting horns to see which ram would be able to mate.

Much of the two men's dislike for each other showed in their body language, but some showed in the tone of their words to each other.

"Why not use the word 'ships' instead of 'sheeps'?" Boyet asked. "We are no sheep, you sweet lamb, unless we feed on your lips."

"You sheep, and I pastor," Maria said. "Shall that finish the jest?"

"So long as you grant pasture for me," Boyet said, moving to kiss her.

Maria stopped the kiss and said, "Not so, gentle beast. My lips are no common, though several they be."

She was punning. A common is pastureland held in common; any citizen can use it. Pastureland that is referred to as several, however, is privately owned. It is severed — separate — from common land. Maria was saying that her lips were privately owned, by herself, and they were several — more than one.

"Your lips belong to whom?" Boyet asked.

"To my fortunes and me," Maria said.

"Good wits will be jangling, aka squabbling," the Princess said, "but, gentlefolk, agree that this civil war of wits would be much better used on the King of Navarre and his fellow book-men; for here such verbal wrangling is misapplied."

Boyet said, "If my observation, which very seldom lies — that is, is mistaken — of the heart's silent eloquence as disclosed by eyes doesn't deceive me now, the King of Navarre is infected."

"With what?" the Princess asked.

"With that which we lovers title 'affected,'" Boyet replied. "He is in love."

"What is your reason for believing that?" the Princess asked.

"Why, all his powers of expression retired to the court of his eye, peeping through desire — all he could do was to look at you with desire.

"His heart, like an agate, with your print impressed, proud with its form, in his eye pride expressed."

Agate stones were sometimes engraved with the image of a person. Boyet was saying that King Ferdinand's heart was proud because it bore the Princess' image, and this pride was expressed in the King's eyes.

Boyet continued, "His tongue, all impatient to speak and not see, stumbled with haste in his eyesight to be."

In other words, King Ferdinand's tongue was annoyed because it had the power only to speak and was unable to see the Princess' beauty, and so it wanted to be capable of sight. Because of this, King Ferdinand's tongue stumbled when he talked to the Princess because his tongue was metaphorically hurrying to his eyes to share in the eyesight.

Boyet continued, "All senses to that sense — the sense of sight — did make their repair, to feel only through looking on the fairest of fair."

In Boyet's verbal image, all of King Ferdinand's other senses gave primacy to the sense of sight because that is the sense that sees the fairest of fair — the most beautiful of all, who is the Princess. His other senses hoped to share in the sense of sight and to share in the emotion aroused by that sense and so rushed to the King's eyes.

Boyet continued, "It seemed to me that all his senses were locked in his eye, like jewels in crystal for some Prince or Princess to buy, which, tendering their own worth from where they were glassed, did point you to buy them, along as you passed."

Jewels were sometimes carried in a crystal — glass — container so that prosperous buyers could look at them. The King's senses had, in Boyet's visual image, rushed to the crystal of the King's eyes and could now be seen as if they were jewels displayed in a glass container. The Princess could, if she looked, see them, and if she wanted, she could buy and possess them.

Boyet continued, "His face's own margins quoted such amazes that all eyes saw his eyes enchanted with gazes."

In Boyet's verbal image, the King's face was a page in a book. His eyes were the main text, and the rest of his face was the margins. In books of the time, notes appeared in the margins, including the left and right margins, rather than only as footnotes. Often, the notes included arrows pointing to a place in the main text. The rest of the King's face directed attention to the King's eyes, where readers could see that the King was enchanted by seeing the Princess.

Boyet concluded, "I'll give you Aquitaine and all that is his, if you give him for my sake but one loving kiss."

Boyet believed that King Ferdinand was so in love with the Princess that if she gave him only one kiss, he would give her Aquitaine and everything else that belonged to him.

"Let's go to our pavilion," the Princess said. "Boyet is disposed."

She meant that he was disposed to be merry and make jokes.

Boyet said, "I am disposed only to speak that in words which the King's eyes have disclosed. I have only made a mouth of his eye, by adding a tongue that I know will not lie. All I have done is to say in words what the King's eyes were saying in looks."

Rosaline said, "You are an old love-monger — trafficker in love — and you speak skillfully and cleverly."

Maria said, "He is Cupid's grandfather and learns news from Cupid."

Rosaline said, "Then Venus resembles her mother and not her father, for her father is only grim."

Venus, the beautiful and fun-loving goddess of love, was Cupid's mother. If Boyet were Cupid's grandfather, he would be Venus' father. Rosaline meant that Venus must get her beauty from her mother, not from her father.

"Do you hear, my mad wenches?" Boyet asked. "Are you listening to me?"

"No," Maria said.

"Well, then, do you see?" Boyet asked.

He meant this: Do you see what I am trying to tell you?

Rosaline replied, "Yes, we see — our way to be gone."

"You are too hard — too difficult — for me," Boyet replied.

Boyet was a ladies' man, but the ladies had defeated him. He had not succeeded in even getting a kiss.

CHAPTER 3

— 3.1 —

Don Adriano de Armado and Mote, his page, talked together in King Ferdinand's park.

Armado said, "Warble, child; make passionate my sense of hearing."

He wanted Mote to sing a passionate love song.

Mote sang a song titled "Concolinel."

After the song was over, Armado said, "Sweet air! Go, tenderness of years; take this key, give enlargement to the swain, bring him festinately hither. I must employ him in a letter to my love."

As usual, Armado was using fancy language. "Tenderness of years" was a way of referring to the young boy: Mote. The swain was the yokel Costard, and "festinately" meant "quickly" and was derived from the Latin *festina*," which means "hurry."

Mote asked, "Master, will you win your love with a French brawl?"

"How meanest thou?" Armado asked. "Brawling in French?"

Actually, a French brawl was a French dance in which the dancers moved sideways.

"No, my complete master," Mote replied, "but to jig off a tune at the tongue's end, canary to it with your feet, humor it with turning up your eyelids, sigh a note and sing a note, sometimes through the throat, as if you swallowed love with singing love, and sometimes through the nose, as if you snuffed up love by smelling love."

Mote was describing a lover — but an odd lover. This lover would sing a song as if it were a jig — a lively dance. The lover would also dance as he sang — he would move his feet as if he were dancing the dance known as the canary — a lively Spanish dance. At the same time as he was moving his feet, he would sigh a note and sing a note, and sometimes the note would come through his throat and sometimes it would come through his nose.

Mote then began describing the way that Armado ought to dress if he were a stereotypical lover: "Wear your hat penthouse-like over the shop of your eyes; have your arms crossed on your thin-belly doublet like a rabbit on a spit; or your hands in your pocket like a man in imitation of the old painting that I know you have seen."

Shops sometimes had penthouses: projecting roofs. Mote was saying that lovers wore hats with broad brims. They also were thin because they wasted away with longing because they could not eat, and they either kept their arms crossed across their chest or they kept their hands in their pockets. Some painters painted portraits in which the subjects' hands were kept in pockets because hands can be difficult to paint.

Mote continued with an additional detail of how Armado the lover ought to act: "Don't keep too long singing one tune, but sing only a snippet."

Why ought Armado the lover to act this way?

Mote said, "These are lovers' behaviors and manners; these are lovers' moods; these are the things that betray and seduce coy wenches, who would be betrayed and seduced even without these. In addition, these things make them men of note — do you note me? Are you paying attention to me? The men most inclined to do these things become men of reputation."

Armado asked, "How hast thou purchased this experience? How do you know this?"

Mote answered, "By my pennyworth of observation."

Armado began to speak, "But oh —"

Unable to come up with the right words, he repeated himself, "But oh —"

Mote sang a line from a popular song: *"For oh, for oh, the hobby-horse is forgot."*

In some dances, the dancers wore a hobby-horse — a figure of a horse that was attached to their waist. It made a comic image since the dancer appeared to be on horseback. "Hobby-horse" was also slang for "prostitute."

Armado asked, "Callest thou my love a 'hobby-horse'?"

"No, master," Mote replied, "the hobby-horse is only a colt, and your love perhaps is a hackney."

A colt was an uncut — uncastrated — young male horse, but the word "colt" was used to describe a lascivious person of either sex. A "hackney horse" was a horse for hire, and the word "hackney" was slang for "prostitute."

Mote added, "But have you forgotten your love?"

"Almost I had," Armado said.

"Negligent student!" Mote said. "Learn her by heart."

"By heart and in heart, boy."

"And out of heart, master. All those three I will prove."

"What wilt thou prove?" Armado asked.

"I'll prove to be a man, if I live," Mote said. "And now I will prove this: You love her by, in, and without your heart.

"By heart you love her, because your heart cannot come by — possess — her.

"In heart you love her, because your heart is in love with her.

"And out of heart you love her — you are out of heart because you cannot enjoy her."

Armado said, "I am all these three, just as you said."

Mote thought, *And you are three times as much more, and yet nothing at all. You are still a zero.*

Armado ordered Mote, "Fetch hither the swain: Costard. He must deliver a letter for me."

Mote said to himself, "This is a message well sympathized and fittingly contrived; a horse will be ambassador for an ass."

Armado was the ass; the horse was Costard, who would deliver the letter. To be called either an ass or a horse was an insult.

"What sayest thou?" Armado asked.

Mote said, "Indeed, sir, you must send the ass upon the horse, for he is very slow-gaited."

To keep out of trouble, Mote was now referring to Costard as the ass. Because the ass moved slowly, he needed to be sent on horseback to perform his errand of delivering the letter.

Mote said, "But I go now. I ought to leave and get Costard."

"The way is very short. Away! Go!" Armado said.

"I go as swiftly as lead, sir," Mote replied.

"What is your meaning, my pretty ingenious page? Is not lead a metal that is heavy, dull, and slow?"

"*Minime*, honest master; or rather, master, no," Mote replied.

The word "*minime*" is Latin for "not at all."

"I say lead is slow," Armado stated.

"You are too swift, sir, to say so," Mote said. "Is that lead slow which is fired from a gun? Are lead bullets slow?"

"Sweet smoke of rhetoric!" Armado said. "He reputes me a cannon; and the bullet, that's he. I shoot thee at the swain."

"'Bang!' goes the cannon, and away I flee," Mote said.

He exited.

Alone, Armado said to himself, "Mote is a most acute juvenal; he is voluble and free of grace!"

By "juvenal," Armado meant "juvenile," but Mote was also a satirist — a funny critic — like the Roman poet Juvenal.

Armado continued, "By thy favor, sweet welkin, I must sigh in thy face."

The welkin is the sky.

He continued, "Most rude melancholy, valor gives place to thee. I am now melancholy rather than valorous."

He then looked up and said, "My herald is returned."

Mote returned with Costard.

Mote said, "Here is a wonder, master! Here's a costard that has broken a shin."

The word 'costard' meant either an apple or a head, neither of which has a shin — the lower part of a leg.

Armado said, "Here is some enigma, some riddle. Come, thy *l'envoi*; begin."

He was asking for a *l'envoi*, which was the conclusion of a piece of writing and which often explained the writing's moral.

Costard, however, thought that Armado was referring to a treatment for a broken shin.

Costard said, "No egma, no riddle, no *l'envoi*; no salve in the mail, sir. Oh, sir, plantain, a plain plantain! No *l'envoi*, no *l'envoi*; no salve, sir, but a plantain!"

"Egma" was the way Costard pronounced "enigma."

The treatment that Costard wanted was the leaves of the plantain plant. He did not want what he thought were the treatments called egma, riddle, *l'envoi*, and salve in the mail — a mail was a kind of bag.

Knowing that Costard was mistaken about the meaning of *l'envoi*, Armado said, "By my virtue, thou enforcest laughter; thy silly thought affects my spleen; the heaving of my lungs provokes me to ridiculous smiling. Oh, pardon me, my stars! Doth the inconsiderate take salve for *l'envoi*, and the word '*l'envoi*' for a salve?"

Mote asked, "Do the wise think them to be otherwise? Is not *l'envoi* a salve?"

L'envoi was a written conclusion, or an author's farewell. The Latin word "*salve,*" which has two syllables, was used both as a greeting and as a farewell.

"No, page," Armado said. "The word '*l'envoi*' is an epilogue or discourse, to make plain some obscure precedence that has tofore been sain."

The archaic word "sain" meant "said," but the word "written" was the right word and it should have been used. The archaic word "tofore" meant "earlier."

Armado said, "I will example it: The fox, the ape, and the humble-bee, were still at odds, being but three. There's the moral. Now the *l'envoi*."

Mote said, "I will add the *l'envoi*. Say the moral again."

Armado repeated, "The fox, the ape, and the humble-bee, were still at odds, being but three."

Mote said, "Until the goose came out of door, and ended the odds by adding number four."

Mote then said, "Now I will begin with your moral, and you follow the moral with my *l'envoi*."

He said the moral: "The fox, the ape, and the humble-bee, were still at odds, being but three."

Armado said, "Until the goose came out of door, ending the odds by adding number four."

Mote said, "This is a good *l'envoi* because it ends in the goose."

The French word for "goose" is *oie*, which is the same sound as the ending of *l'envoi*. The joke had ended with Armado saying the word "goose" — the end of the joke was "goose," aka Armado.

Mote asked, "Would you desire more?"

Costard, realizing that Mote had called Armado a goose, aka a fool, said, "The boy has sold him a bargain, a goose, that's flat."

A person who has been sold a bargain has been made a fool of.

Costard said to Mote, "Sir, your pennyworth is good, if your goose be fat. To sell a bargain well is as cunning as the con game called fast and loose. Let me see, a fat *l'envoi* — aye, that's a fat goose."

Armado said, "Come hither, come hither. How did this conversation begin?"

Mote replied, "It began by saying that a costard had broken a shin, and then you called for the *l'envoi*."

"True," Costard said, "and then I called for plantain leaves. Then came in the rest of the conversation: the boy's fat *l'envoi*, the goose that you bought; and he ended the market."

A proverb of the time stated, "Three women and a goose make a market." Once the goose is sold, the market is over.

Armado asked, "But tell me; how was there a costard broken in a shin?"

Mote said, "I will tell you sensibly."

By "sensibly," Mote meant, "in an easily understandable and commonsense way," but Costard misunderstood "sensibly" to mean "with real emotion."

Costard objected, "You have no feeling of it, Mote. I will speak that *l'envoi*: I, Costard, running out, that was safely within, fell over the threshold and broke my shin."

One interpretation of Costard's words is that as he was running from inside a building to outside the building, he tripped on the threshold and hurt his shin.

But the words supported another interpretation: Costard was having sex, he ejaculated — his semen ran out of his penis as it was safely inside a vagina — but as he attempted one additional thrust his penis slipped out and was injured at the threshold — entrance — of the vagina. He thrust, missed the opening of the vagina, and bent his penis. In this interpretation, Costard's penis is a third leg.

Armado said, "We will talk no more of this matter."

Costard replied, "Until there be more matter — pus — in the injured shin."

Armado said, "Sirrah Costard, I will enfranchise thee."

Costard misunderstood; he thought that Armado had said, "Sirrah Costard, I will in-Frances thee."

In this society, "Frances" was a common name for prostitutes.

Costard replied, "Oh, marry me to one Frances: I smell some *l'envoi*, some goose, in this."

"Goose" was a slang word for "prostitute."

Armado said, "By my sweet soul, I mean setting thee at liberty, enfreedoming thy person; thou wert immured, restrained, captivated, bound."

Costard replied, "True, true; and now you will be my purgation and let me loose."

One interpretation of this exchange, of course, is Costard was bound in prison and now Armado was going to clear — purge — him of his crime and set him loose.

But the words supported another interpretation: Costard's bowels were bound up — he was constipated. Armado was going to purge him — give him a laxative. This would loosen Costard's bowels so that he could defecate.

Armado said, "I give thee thy liberty, set thee free from durance; and, in lieu thereof, impose on thee nothing but this: Bear this significant to the country maid Jaquenetta."

The "significant" was a letter that he gave to Costard.

Armado gave Costard some money and said, "Here is remuneration; for the best ward of mine honor is rewarding my dependents."

"The best ward of mine honor is rewarding my dependents" meant "The best way to defend my honor is to reward my servants."

Armado ordered, "Mote, follow," and then he exited.

Mote said, "Like the sequel, I follow. Signior Costard, adieu."

Costard said, "My sweet ounce of man's flesh! My incony Jew!"

"Incony" meant "darling," and "Jew" was Costard's way of shortening "juvenile."

Mote exited.

Alone, Costard said to himself, "Now will I look to his remuneration. Remuneration! Oh, that's the Latin word for 'three farthings': 'three farthings' equals a 'remuneration.'"

A farthing was worth one quarter of a penny.

Costard continued, "I will say, 'What's the price of this inkle — this linen yarn?'

"Back comes the reply, 'One penny.'

"I will bargain and say, 'No, I'll give you a remuneration.'

"Why, it carries it away and wins the day. Remuneration! Why, it is a fairer name than 'French crown.' I will never buy and sell without using this word."

Biron walked over to Costard and said, "Oh, my good knave Costard! We are exceedingly well met."

"Please, sir," Costard said, "how much carnation-colored ribbon may a man buy for a remuneration?"

"What is a remuneration?" Biron asked.

"Indeed, sir, it is a halfpenny farthing."

A halfpenny was worth two farthings, and a halfpenny farthing was worth three farthings.

"Why, then, three farthings' worth of silk," Biron said.

"I thank your worship," Costard said. "May God be with you!"

Costard started to leave, and Biron said, "Stay, rascal. I must employ thee on an errand. If you want to win my favor, my good knave, do one thing for me that I shall entreat you to do."

"When would you have it done, sir?" Costard asked.

"This afternoon."

"Well, I will do it, sir," Costard said. "Fare you well."

Again, he started to leave, but Biron said, "You don't know what it is that I want you to do."

"I shall know, sir, when I have done it," Costard replied.

"Why, villain, you must know first what I want done."

"I will come to your worship tomorrow morning to find out."

"It must be done this afternoon," Biron said. "Listen, rascal, what I want you to do is only this: The Princess comes to hunt here in the park, and in her train there is a noble lady; when tongues speak sweetly, then they name her name, and Rosaline they call her. Ask for her, and to her white hand see that you hand over this sealed confidential letter."

This society valued pale skin and so Biron flattered Rosaline by referring to what he called her "white hand." But Rosaline was the darkest of the three women — Rosaline, Maria, and Katherine — and for many people in this society that made her the ugliest of the three.

He handed Costard the letter and a shilling and said, "There's the letter and your guerdon; now go."

A shilling is worth twelve pence, so Biron had tipped much more generously than Armado.

Mispronouncing "guerdon," which means "reward," Costard said, "Gardon! Oh, sweet gardon! Better than remuneration! It is eleven-pence farthing better! Most sweet gardon!"

"*Gardon*" is French for "cockroach."

Eleven-pence farthing plus three farthings equals twelve pence. Biron's guerdon of twelve-pence was eleven-pence farthing more than Armado's remuneration of three farthings.

Costard said to Biron, "I will do your errand, sir, in print. I will do it to the letter. Gardon! Remuneration!"

Costard exited.

Alone, Biron said to himself, "And I, indeed, am in love! I, who have been love's whip, a very beadle to a lovesick sigh, a censurer, nay, a night-watch constable, a domineering pedantic schoolmaster over the boy Cupid, than whom no mortal is as arrogant and proud!"

Biron was saying that he had always kept tight control of himself when it came to love. He had been like a beadle or a night-watch constable who caught prostitutes and gave them their legal punishment of a whipping. He, Biron, had been the adult master of the boy Cupid.

Biron continued, "Cupid is this blindfolded, whining, completely blind, wayward boy."

Cupid was often depicted blindfolded because love is blind.

Biron continued, "He is this senior-junior, this giant-dwarf, this Dan Cupid."

Cupid was senior and junior; he was the oldest and the youngest of gods. Love had brought order out of chaos at the beginning of the world, and so Cupid was the most senior god. However, Cupid was always depicted as a young boy, and so he was also the most junior of the gods.

Cupid was depicted as a boy, but as the god of love, he had much power. And so he was a "giant-dwarf."

"Dan Cupid" meant "Don Cupid." "Don" was a respectful title meaning "sir."

Biron continued, "Cupid is the regent of love-rhymes, the lord of folded arms, the anointed sovereign of sighs and groans, the liege of all loiterers and malcontents, the dread Prince of plackets, the King of codpieces, sole Imperator and great General of trotting apparitors."

Male lovers were stereotypically depicted with folded arms or with their hands in their pockets. Plackets were literally openings in ladies' petticoats and therefore metaphorically referred to female genitalia. A codpiece was literally a pouch that was fitted to a man's breeches and which covered the genitals and therefore metaphorically referred to male genitalia. Apparitors were legal officers who summoned sex offenders to appear in court.

Biron continued, "Oh, my little heart! And I am to be a Corporal of his field, and wear his regimental colors like an acrobat's hoop with its brightly colored ribbons!

"What, I! I love! I woo! I seek a wife!

"A woman is like a German clock, very complex and breaking, always being repaired, forever out of order, and never going right, being a watch, but needing to be watched so that it may still go right!"

Biron's view of women was poor: Women needed to be constantly watched lest they commit adultery.

Biron continued, "Because I am in love, I will be perjured, which is worst of all; I will break my vow.

"And, among the three women — Rosaline, Maria, and Katherine — I love the worst of all. She is wightly — unfortunately — wanton with a forehead as soft and smooth as velvet, with two pitch-black balls stuck in her face for eyes. Yes, and by Heaven, she is one who will do the deed and have illicit sex even though Argus the hundred-eyed monster were her eunuch and her guard."

Eunuchs — castrated men — were used to guard harems in some societies to avoid any chance of the guards sleeping with members of the harem.

Biron continued, "And I to sigh for her! To stay awake at night so that I can watch her lest she commit adultery! To pray for her!

"Bah! This is a plague that Cupid will impose on me to punish me for my neglect of his almighty dreadful little might.

"Well, I will love, write, sigh, pray, woo, and groan.

"Some men must love my lady, and some men must love Joan."

"Joan" was used to refer to a lower-class woman. Biron had in mind the proverb "Joan is as good as my lady in the dark." "My lady" was used to refer to an upper-class woman.

Biron was in love, but he honestly felt that he was in love with the worst of the three women the Princess had brought with her from France.

Why would he think this? After all, he hardly knows her and he hardly knows anything about her.

Boyet is the reason. Boyet had managed to convey the impression in a very brief conversation that he had slept with Rosaline.

45

CHAPTER 4

— 4.1 —

The Princess was going hunting in King Ferdinand's park. With her was her train of attendants and a forester, as well as Boyet, Rosaline, Maria, and Katherine.

The Princess asked, "Was that the King — that man whom we saw spurring his horse so hard up the virtually perpendicular hill?"

"I don't know," Boyet replied, "but I don't think it was he."

"Whoever he was, he showed a mounting mind," the Princess said.

Members of this society enjoyed joking about sex, and some of her listeners may have thought about a man mounting a woman.

The Princess continued, "Well, lords, today we shall have our dispatch: We will have completed our diplomatic mission and will have official leave to go. On Saturday we will return to France."

"So then, forester, my friend, where is the bush where we must stand and play the murderer in?"

Part of the official entertainment for the Princess was hunting deer. She was being taken to a place from which she could shoot an arrow at a deer. Although she did not care for hunting, part of being a good guest and ambassador involved participating in the entertainment arranged by the host.

The forester replied, "Nearby, upon the edge of yonder coppice of trees, is the stand — the hunter's station —where you may make the fairest shoot."

The fairest shoot was the best shot, but the Princess deliberately misinterpreted the words "fairest shoot" in part to mean "the most beautiful growing thing."

She said, "I thank my beauty. I am fair and I am alive and growing and I shoot, and because of that you speak about the fairest shoot."

"Pardon me, madam, for I did not mean it that way," the forester said.

He did not want the Princess to think that he, a commoner, was flirting with her.

"What! What!" The Princess was in a joking mood. "First you praise me and then you take it back! Oh, short-lived pride! I am not fair! I am not beautiful! Alas and woe!"

"Yes, madam, you are fair," the forester said. "You are beautiful."

"Nay, never flatter me now," the Princess said. "Where fair beauty is not, flattering praise cannot mend the brow and make a face beautiful. Here, my good and honest looking-glass, take this for telling the truth."

She handed him some money and said, "Fair payment for foul words is more than due."

"Nothing but fair is that which you have," the forester said.

"See! See! My beauty will be saved by merit!" the Princess said. "Oh, heresy in fair, fit for these days! A giving hand, though foul, shall have fair praise."

Roman Catholics believed that merit, such as that gotten by doing good works, was important in achieving salvation, in contrast to Protestants, who emphasized the importance of faith. The Princess' merit was giving the forester a tip, and that had achieved salvation for her beauty — after receiving the tip, the forester had said that she is beautiful.

The Princess then said, "But come, the bow. Now mercy goes to kill, and shooting well is then accounted ill."

Although she preferred to be merciful and not kill a deer, part of her duty as ambassador was to hunt; unfortunately, if she shot well and killed a deer, it would be ill for her reputation as a person who was merciful.

The Princess continued, "Thus will I save my reputation in the shoot. Not wounding, I will say that pity would not let me do it; if wounding, then I will say that it was to show my skill."

If she missed the deer, she could say that she felt pity for it and so she had missed on purpose so that she would not hurt it. If her arrow hit the deer, then she could say that she had shot the deer in order to demonstrate her skill at archery.

She continued, "If I kill the deer, I can say that more for praise than purpose I meant to kill, and it is no question that sometimes the thirst for glory leads us to grow guilty of detested crimes, as when, for fame's sake, for praise, an outward part, we bend to that the working of the heart, as I for praise alone now seek to spill the blood of a poor deer that my heart means no ill."

If she would shoot the deer in order to show her skill, she would be shooting the deer in order to gain glory. In the Princess' opinion, causing the deer pain and taking the deer's life only in order to gain glory was a detestable sin.

Boyet said, "Don't curst wives hold that self-sovereignty only for praise's sake, when they strive to be lords over their lords?"

He was asking whether shrewish wives ordered their husbands around, rather than vice versa, only to gain praise.

The Princess answered, "Yes, they do it only for praise, and praise we may give to any lady who subdues a lord."

"Here comes a member of the commonwealth," Boyet said. "Here comes a citizen of this country."

Costard walked over to the group and said, "May God give you all a good evening! Please, which of you is the head lady?"

"You shall know her, fellow, by the rest who have no heads," the Princess said.

She may have been joking that Rosaline, Maria, and Katherine had no maidenheads — they were no longer virgins.

"Which is the greatest lady, the highest?" Costard asked.

"The greatest lady, the highest, is the thickest and the tallest," the Princess said.

The thickest lady is the lady with the biggest waist.

"The thickest and the tallest!" Costard said. "It is so; truth is truth. If your waist, mistress, were as slender as my wit, one of these maidens' girdles for your waist should be fit. Aren't you the chief woman? You are the thickest here."

"What's your will, sir?" the Princess asked. "What do you want?"

Costard replied, "I have a letter from Monsieur Biron to one Lady Rosaline."

"Oh, your letter, your letter!" the Princess said, delighted and curious to know the contents of the letter. "Biron is a good friend of mine."

She took a letter from Costard and said, "Stand aside, good letter bearer."

Then she said, "Boyet, you can carve; break up this capon."

A capon is a castrated rooster, aka cock, that has been fattened for the dinner table, but a capon is also a love letter. According to E. Cobham Brewer's *Dictionary of Phrase and Fable* (1894), a capon is "A love-letter. In French, *poulet* means not only a chicken but also a love-letter, or a sheet of note-paper. Thus Henri IV., consulting with Sully about his marriage, says: 'My niece of Guise would please me best, though report says maliciously that she loves poulets in paper better than in a fricasee.'"

To break up this capon meant to open the letter.

Of course, the Princess had witnessed the mean-spirited exchange of words between Boyet and Biron earlier. Remembering that may have caused her to think of a castrated cock when hearing of a love letter from Biron to Rosaline, and to refer to the letter in that way when asking Boyet to read it.

Boyet replied, "I am bound to serve."

He looked at the letter and said, "This letter has been delivered to the wrong place; it concerns no one here. This letter is written to a woman named Jaquenetta."

"We will read it, I swear," the Princess said. "Break the neck of the wax, and every one give ear."

"Break the neck of the wax" meant "Break the wax seal and open the letter," but the Princess also had in mind breaking the neck of the capon, aka *poulet*.

Boyet read the letter, which was by Armado to Jaquenetta, out loud:

"*By Heaven, that thou art fair, is most infallible; it is true that thou art beauteous; it is truth itself that thou art lovely. Thou, who are more fairer than fair, beautiful than beauteous, truer than truth itself, have commiseration on thy heroical vassal!*"

By "commiseration," Armado meant "mercy."

Boyet continued reading Armado's letter to Jaquenetta out loud:

"*The magnanimous and most illustrate King Cophetua set eye upon the pernicious and indubitate beggar Zenelophon.*"

By "illustrate," Armado meant "illustrious." By the phrase "pernicious and indubitate," Armado meant "indubitably penurious" or "definitely impoverished" — "pernicious" was a malapropism for "penurious." In this passage, he was comparing himself to King Cophetua and Jaquenetta to the beggar Zenelophon; in fact, Armado had a higher social status than Jaquenetta.

Boyet continued reading Armado's letter to Jaquenetta out loud:

"*And he it was that might rightly say,* Veni, vidi, vici; *which to annothanize in the vulgar, common language — oh, base and obscure vulgar! —* videlicet, *He came, see, and overcame: he came, one; see, two; overcame, three.*"

Videlicet is Latin for "namely." Julius Caesar wrote the words "*Veni, vidi, vici,*" which mean "I came, I saw, I conquered." Armado had a fondness for archaisms, and so he wrote the archaic past tense "I see" rather than the modern "I saw."

By "annothanize," Armado may have meant one or more of these meanings: "anatomize, explain, interpret, gloss, annotate."

Boyet continued reading Armado's letter to Jaquenetta out loud:

"*Who came? The King. Why did he come? To see. Why did he see? To overcome. To whom came he? To the beggar. What saw he? The beggar. Who overcame he? The beggar. The conclusion is victory. On whose side? The King's. The captive is enriched. On whose side? The beggar's. The catastrophe is a nuptial. On whose side? The King's. No, on both in one, or one in both. I am the King; for so stands the comparison: thou are the beggar; for so witnesseth thy lowliness.*"

The word "catastrophe" means "denouement or outcome."

Boyet continued reading Armado's letter to Jaquenetta out loud:

"*Shall I command thy love? I may. Shall I enforce thy love? I could. Shall I entreat thy love? I will.*"

"To enforce thy love" means "to rape."

Boyet continued reading Armado's letter to Jaquenetta out loud:

"*What shalt thou exchange for rags? Robes. For tittles? Titles. For thyself? Me. Thus, expecting thy reply, I profane my lips on thy foot, my eyes on thy picture, and my heart on thy every part. Thine, in the dearest design of industry,*

"*Signed, DON ADRIANO DE ARMADO.*"

"Tittles" are tiny, insignificant things.

By "the dearest design of industry," Armado meant "the most heartfelt undertaking of assiduous service to a lady."

Boyet continued reading Armado's letter to Jaquenetta out loud:

"*Thus dost thou hear the Nemean lion roar 'gainst thee, thou lamb, that standest as his prey. Submissive fall his Princely feet before, and he from forage will incline to play. But if thou strive, poor soul, what art thou then? Food for his rage, repasture for his den.*"

The Nemean lion is the lion that Hercules killed as the first of his famous labors. Armado was referring to himself as the lion, and to Jaquenetta as the lion's prey. The word "repasture" meant "repast"; in this case, it meant a meal in the lion's den.

The Princess asked, "What plume of feathers is he who composed this letter? What weathervane? What weathercock? Did you ever hear better?"

A plume of feathers is metaphorically a showoff — someone who is capable of wearing feathers so that he will stand out. A weathervane is metaphorically a man who is very changeable — who constantly turns and changes similar to the way that a weathervane turns and changes with the wind. In referring to "weathervane," the Princess was also punning on "vain."

Boyet said, "I am much deceived if I do not remember the style."

He meant that he remembered Armado using the same style in his speech as he had used in his letter.

"Or else your memory is bad, since you just read the letter and ought to remember its style," the Princess said.

Boyet said, "This Armado is a Spaniard, who resides here in court; he is a phantasime, a Monarcho, and one who provides entertainment for the Prince — King Ferdinand — and his fellow bookmates."

A phantasime is a person who behaves extravagantly.

Monarcho was the name of an insane Italian who entertained Queen Elizabeth I in her court; he believed that he was Emperor of the World.

The Princess said to Costard, "Fellow, I want a word with you. Who gave you this letter?"

"I told you," Costard said. "My lord did."

"To whom should you have given it?"

"From my lord to my lady."

"From which lord to which lady?" the Princess asked.

"From my lord Biron, a good master of mine, to a lady of France whom he called Rosaline."

"You have taken his letter to the wrong person," the Princess said, but she did not return the letter to him.

She said, "Come, lords, away."

She gave the letter to Rosaline and said, "Here, sweet, put this away. It will be your turn to receive a love letter some other day."

The Princess and a train of her attendants exited.

Boyet asked Rosaline, "Who is the suitor? Who is the suitor?"

He was teasing her by asking who was wooing her and would send her a love letter, but he pronounced "suitor" almost exactly like "shooter."

"Shall I teach you to know?" Rosaline asked.

"Yes, my container of beauty," Boyet replied.

"Why, she who bears the bow," Rosaline said, adding, "I have finely put off — avoided — your query!"

"My lady goes to kill horns," Boyet said, "but, if you marry, hang me by the neck if horns that year miscarry —if they are in short supply."

By "My lady goes to kill horns," Boyet meant that his lady boss, the Princess, had left to shoot and kill a horned deer.

The other kind of horns were the horns of a cuckold; when a man had a cheating wife who cuckolded him, horns were said to grow on the man's head. Boyet was joking that if Rosaline were to marry, there would be no lack of horns because she would be busy cuckolding her husband with many men.

He then said, "Finely put on — a hit! My insult has found its target!"

Rosaline said, "Well, then, I am the shooter."

"And who is your deer?" Boyet asked.

"If we choose by the horns, yourself come not near," Rosaline said.

She was deliberating mistaking "deer" as "dear" and rejecting Boyet as her dear because, she joked, he was the type of husband she would cuckold and make grow horns.

She then said, "Finely put on, indeed! My insult has found its target!"

Maria said, "You always wrangle and combat verbally with her, Boyet, and she strikes at the brow."

The brow, aka forehead, is where the horns of the cuckold grow; Rosaline had aimed her comic insult at Boyet's brow.

"But she herself is hit lower," Boyet replied. "Have I hit her now?"

A woman's vagina is a lower target than a cuckold's brow. For that target to be hit, the head of a penis must enter it the way the head of an arrow must enter the center of a target.

Rosaline replied, "Shall I come upon thee with an old saying that was a man — that was mature — when King Pepin of France, Charlemagne's father, who died in 768 A.D., was a little boy, as touching the 'hit it'?"

Pepin the Short (*le Bref*) of France had a sister named Bellysant who was married to Alexander, the Emperor of Greece; she was falsely accused of adultery and gave birth to twin boys: Valentine and Orson.

Boyet answered, "As long as I may answer you with one as old, that was a woman — that was mature — when Queen Guinevere of Britain was a little wench, as touching the 'hit it.'"

Queen Guinevere of Britain was famous for cuckolding her husband, King Arthur, who himself was famous for his Knights of the Round Table.

Rosaline began to sing a popular song:

"*Thou canst not hit it, hit it, hit it,*

"*Thou canst not hit it, my good man.*"

In other words, you, Boyet, cannot put your penis in my vagina.

Boyet then sang the next two lines:

"*If I cannot, cannot, cannot,*

"*If I cannot, another can.*"

Rosaline then exited.

Costard had enjoyed the verbal joking: "I swear that was most pleasant. How both did fit it!"

Both had fit the song; they had harmonized well together.

Another meaning was that they fit well together, just like a penis in a vagina.

Maria said, "That was a mark marvelously well shot, for they both did hit it."

The mark is a target; the target for many men is a vagina.

Boyet said, "A mark! Oh, mark but that mark! A mark, says my lady! Let the mark have a prick in it, to aim at, if it may be."

In archery, the prick is a bull's-eye. In another kind of sport, it is a penis.

"You are wide of the bow hand," Maria said. "Your hand is out."

The bow hand is, usually, the left hand; it is the hand that holds the bow. Maria meant that Boyet had missed the bull's-eye by shooting to the left of it.

Costard said, "Indeed, he must shoot nearer, or he'll never hit the clout."

The clout is a pin fixing a target; here it meant a pin in the center of the bull's-eye. One kind of shooting is ejaculation.

When Maria had said, "Your hand is out," she meant, "You are out of practice."

Boyet took the meaning in another sense in his answer: "Your hand is out" equals "Your hand is out of the vagina."

He said to Maria, "If my hand is out, then it is likely that your hand is in."

In other words, if I am not fingering you, it is probably because you are masturbating.

Costard said, "Then she will get the upshoot by cleaving the pin."

One meaning of "upshoot" is "best shot," and one meaning of "cleaving" is "splitting." Costard meant, "Then Maria will get the best shot by shooting the arrow accurately and splitting the pin at the very center of the target.

But "upshoot," "cleaving," and "pin" have other meanings. Another meaning of "cleaving" was "holding fast to."

Using the other meanings, Costard had said this: "Then she will get the man to ejaculate by firmly holding his penis."

Maria, and the other women in this society, knew these and other double entendres.

She said, "Come, come, you talk greasily; your lips grow foul."

"To talk greasily" is to "talk in a vulgar way."

Costard said to Boyet, "She's too hard for you at pricks, sir. Challenge her to bowl instead."

One meaning was this: "Maria is too hard for you to beat at archery, sir. Challenge her to a game of bowling instead."

Another interpretation was this: "Maria is making it too hard for you to beat her at the game of pricks — she won't allow you to use your prick, sir. Challenge her to a game of bowling instead."

In the game of lawn bowling, the bowl — the ball — sometimes met an obstacle. This was called rubbing. Rubbing was also a word to use to refer to masturbation and sex.

Boyet replied, "I fear too much rubbing. Good night, my good owl — my wise person."

Boyet and Maria exited.

Alone, Costard said to himself, "By my soul, a swain — a yokel! A most simple clown!"

He was referring to Boyet.

Costard continued, "Lord, Lord, how the ladies and I have put him down! I swear, these were very sweet jests! Most incony and daring vulgar wit! When it comes so smoothly off, so obscenely, as it were, it is so fitting."

Costard then compared Boyet to Armado and Mote; he thought that Boyet had the manners of Armado and the wit of Mote, so on one side Boyet was Armado and on the other side he was Mote — and Costard took pride in helping the French ladies defeat such a man as Boyet.

"Armado, on the other hand — oh, he is a most dainty man! To see him walk before a lady and to bear her fan! To see him kiss his hand! And how most sweetly he will swear!

"And his page — Mote — on the other hand, that handful of wit!

"Ah, Heavens, Boyet is a most pathetic little fellow! And I and the ladies have defeated him!"

Hearing the sounds of hunting, Costard cried, "Sola! Sola!"

This was a hunting cry, and he ran off to join the hunting party.

Holofernes the schoolmaster, Sir Nathaniel the curate, and Dull the constable talked together in King Ferdinand's park.

A curate is a member of the clergy; it is proper to call a curate "Sir."

Holofernes is the name of Gargantua's tutor in *Gargantua and Pantagruel*, Rabelais' satiric masterpiece. Rabelais died in 1553.

Referring to the hunting of deer, Sir Nathaniel said, "It is a very reverend and very worthy sport, truly; and it is done in the testimony — with the warrant — of a good conscience."

2 Corinthians 1:12 reads, "*For our rejoicing is this, the testimony of our conscience, that in simplicity and godly pureness, and not in fleshly wisdom, but by the grace of God we have had our conversation in the world, and most of all to youwards*" (1599 Geneva Bible).

Holofernes said about the deer that the Princess had shot, "The deer was, as you know, *sanguis*, in blood; ripe as the pomewater apple, which now hangeth like a jewel in the ear of *caelo*, the sky, the welkin, the Heaven; and anon, soon, falleth like a crab apple on the face of *terra*, the soil, the land, the earth."

As a schoolmaster, Holofernes showed off his knowledge by using many Latin words. For example, *caelo* is, as he said, the sky, and *terra* is, as he said, earth or land. Sometimes, he made a mistake. For example, "in blood" ought to be "*sanguine*" in Latin.

He also used strings of many synonyms in his conversation. For example, "*caelo*, the sky, the welkin, the Heaven."

"Truly, Master Holofernes," Sir Nathaniel said, "the epithets are sweetly varied, like a scholar to say the least, but, sir, I assure ye, it was a buck of the first head."

Holofernes had called the animal the Princess had shot a deer, but Sir Nathaniel was more specific when he called it a buck, especially when he called it a buck of the first head — a male deer that was five years old and had its first set of antlers.

Holofernes replied, "Sir Nathaniel, *haud credo*."

"*Haud credo*" is Latin for "I don't believe it," but Constable Dull misunderstood and thought that Holofernes was saying that the deer was an auld grey doe. "Auld" was a way of saying "old" in Constable Dull's dialect, and so he thought that perhaps "*haud credo*" was Holofernes' way of pronouncing "auld grey doe."

Constable Dull said, "It was not a *haud credo*, aka an auld grey doe; it was a pricket."

A pricket is a two-year-old buck.

"Most barbarous intimation!" Holofernes said. "Yet a kind of insinuation, as it were, *in via*, in a way, of explication; *facere*, to make, as it were, replication, an echo, or rather, *ostentare*, to show, as it were, his inclination, after — that is, according to — his undressed and unfinished, unpolished, uneducated, unpruned, untrained, or rather, unlettered, or ratherest, unconfirmed and inexperienced fashion, to insert again my *haud credo* for a deer."

An "intimation" is an "announcement," and an "insinuation" is a "suggestion."

Holofernes was saying that Constable Dull had made a very barbarous announcement that was a suggestion — a suggestion that used Holofernes' own words of *haud credo* — and mistakenly thought that they referred to a particular type of deer.

Constable Dull repeated, "I said the deer was not an auld grey doe; it was a two-year-old buck — it was a pricket."

Holofernes said, "Twice-sod simplicity, *bis coctus*!"

"Twice-sod" meant "twice soaked," and "*bis coctus*" is Latin for "twice cooked."

Holofernes continued, "Oh, thou monster Ignorance, how deformed dost thou look!"

Sir Nathaniel said, "Sir, he has never fed on the dainties that are bred in a book; he has not eaten paper, as it were; he has not drunk ink: his intellect is not replenished; he is only an animal, only sensible in the duller parts. And such barren plants are set before us, that we thankful should be, which we who of taste and feeling are, for those parts that do fructify — grow fruitful — in us more than in him.

"For as it would ill become me to be vain, indiscreet, or a fool, so we see a patch set on learning, if we were to see him in a school."

Holofernes believed that he and Sir Nathaniel were much more intelligent than Constable Dull, whom Holofernes considered to be a patch, aka fool.

Anyone who saw Constable Dull in a school would, according to Holofernes, know that a fool was being made to attend lessons.

"But *omne bene*, say I — all's well. Being of a wise old father's mind, I say that many can brook — endure — the weather who love not the wind."

In other words, what can't be cured must be endured.

Sir Nathaniel was saying that Holofernes and he could not stop Constable Dull from being a fool, but they could endure him.

Constable Dull wanted to show them that he was intelligent, so he asked them a riddle: "You two are book-men. Can you use your wit and tell me what was a month old when Cain, a son of Adam of Garden of Eden fame, was born, but is not five weeks old as of now?"

Holofernes knew the answer: "Dictynna, goodman Dull; Dictynna, goodman Dull."

Constable Dull asked, "What is Dictynna?"

Sir Nathaniel answered, "A title for Phoebe, for Luna, for the Moon."

This is correct; Dictynna is an obscure title used by the Roman poet Ovid for the Moon-goddess. Dictynna, aka Britomartis, was a Cretan hunter-goddess, and Ovid identified her with the Greek hunter-goddess Artemis, whom the Romans identified with Diana, the Moon-goddess.

Holofernes said, "The Moon was a month old when Adam was no more than a month old, and the Moon did not reach five weeks old when Adam came to the age of five-score: one hundred. The allusion holds in the exchange."

By "allusion" Holofernes meant "riddle." The exchange was the exchange of the names Cain and Adam — the riddle worked no matter which name you used. In addition, Holofernes was making wordplay on the changes of the Moon.

Constable Dull said, "It is true indeed; the collusion holds in the exchange."

Dull meant to say "allusion," but it was true that Sir Nathaniel and Holofernes were colluding together in the exchange of conversation to show that they — in their opinion — were intellectually superior to Constable Dull.

Holofernes said, "God comfort thy capacity! May God strengthen your intelligence and understanding. I say, the allusion holds in the exchange."

Constable Dull said, "And I say, the pollution holds in the exchange; for the Moon is never but a month old, and I say besides that, it was a two-year-old buck — a pricket — that the Princess killed."

Again, Dull meant to say "allusion," but "pollution" was an apt word to describe the language of Sir Nathaniel and Holofernes. Certainly, such language was conducive to showing off, but it was not conducive to good communication or good conversation.

Holofernes said, "Sir Nathaniel, will you hear an extemporal and spontaneous epitaph on the death of the deer? And, to humor the ignorant, I will call the deer that the Princess killed a pricket."

Sir Nathaniel replied, "*Perge*, good Master Holofernes, *perge* — provided that it shall please you to abrogate scurrility."

Perge is Latin for "proceed." "To abrogate scurrility" meant "to avoid scandalous language" — Sir Nathaniel was worried about the word "pricket."

Holofernes said, "I will somewhat affect the letter — achieve alliteration — for it argues facility with language."

He paused and then said, "The preyful Princess pierced and pricked a pretty pleasing pricket."

"Preyful" meant "killing much prey."

Holofernes continued, "Some say a sore; but not a sore, until now made sore with shooting."

A sore is a four-year-old buck. Holofernes was saying that the buck was not a sore until it became sore after being shot with the Princess' arrow.

Holofernes continued, "The dogs did yell. Add 'L' to 'sore,' and then sorel jumps from thicket."

A sorel is a three-year-old buck.

Holofernes continued, "Either it was a pricket sore, or else a sorel; in either case the people fall a-hooting. If sore be sore, then adding 'L' to 'sore' makes fifty sores of sore L."

"L" is the Roman symbol for "50."

Holofernes continued, "From one sore I a hundred make by adding but one more L. Sore L plus L equals a hundred sores."

Sir Nathaniel was impressed: "That is a rare talent!"

Constable Dull was unimpressed: "If a talent is a claw, look how he claws him with a talent."

For one meaning of "talent," Dull had in mind "talon." Holofernes was impressing Sir Nathaniel with a talent for bad word play and a talent for creating bad extemporaneous alliterative poetry; it was as if Holofernes' 'talent' was a talon clawing Sir Nathaniel.

Holofernes said, "This is a gift that I have — it is simple, simple, and it is a foolish extravagant spirit, full of forms, figures, shapes, objects, ideas, apprehensions, motions and suggestions, revolutions and reflections. These are begot in the ventricle — the hollow depths — of memory, nourished in the womb of the *pia mater*, which is a protective membrane covering the brain, and are delivered, aka given birth to, upon the mellowing of occasion and opportunity. But the gift is good in those in whom it is acute, and I am thankful for it."

Sir Nathaniel said, "Sir, I praise the Lord for you; and so may my parishioners; for their sons are well tutored by you, and their daughters profit very greatly under you. You are a good member of the commonwealth."

Sir Nathaniel, who had been worried about the word "pricket," had just made — unaware — some mistakes of the type he feared. One meaning of "their daughters profit very greatly under you" was "their daughters increase in size — grow pregnant — under you." The word "member" also had a second, sexual meaning.

Holofernes replied, "By Hercules, if their sons be ingenuous and intelligent, they shall want no instruction; if their daughters be capable, I will put it to them."

Again, the passage about daughters had a second, sexual meaning. "Capable" meant "mature," and it also meant "capable of having sex." The phrase "put it to them" also had a second, sexual meaning.

Holofernes then looked up and said, "But *vir sapit qui pauca loquitur*; a soul feminine saluteth us."

"*Vir sapit qui pauca loquitur*" is Latin for "A man is wise who speaks few words."

The "soul feminine" was Jaquenetta, who walked over to Holofernes and Sir Nathaniel. She was accompanied by Costard.

Jaquenetta said to Sir Nathaniel, "May God give you a good morning, master Person."

"Person" was her pronunciation of "Parson."

Holofernes said, "Master Person, *quasi* pierce-one?"

"*Quasi*" is Latin for "as if" or "as if it were."

Holofernes continued, "If one should be pierced, which is the one?"

Costard answered, "Indeed, master schoolmaster, he who is most like a hogshead."

A hogshead is a barrel. A barrel of wine is tapped — pierced — in order to get the wine out of the barrel.

"Piercing a hogshead!" Holofernes said. "That is a good luster of conceit in a tuft of earth."

"A good luster of conceit" is "a good spark of imagination," and "a tuft of earth" is a "clod." Holofernes regarded Costard as a clod, but he enjoyed Costard's joke.

Holofernes said about the joke, "It is fire enough for a flint, and pearl enough for a swine. It is pretty; it is well."

He was thinking of two proverbs: "In the coldest flint there is hot fire" and "Cast not pearls before swine."

This time using the correct pronunciation of "Parson," Jaquenetta said, "Good master Parson, be so good as to read this letter to me. It was given to me by Costard, and sent to me from Don Armado. I beseech you, read it."

She gave the letter to Sir Nathaniel, who began to read it.

Holofernes had heard Jaquenetta say, "I beseech you," meaning, "Please." He now launched into a quotation using the Latin word "*precor*," which means "I beseech" or "I ask."

He said, "'*Facile precor gelida quando peccas omnia sub umbra ruminat*' — and so forth."

The Latin means, more or less, "Easily, I pray, since you are making a mess of everything in the cool shade. It ruminates [...]."

The Latin quotation is inaccurate. The correct quotation is this: "*Fauste, precor gelida quando pecus omne sub umbra ruminat.*"

The Latin means, "Faustus, since your whole flock is ruminating in the cool shade, I pray [...]."

The Latin quotation is the first few words of the first poem in the *Eclogues*, published in 1498. Johannes Baptista Spagnolo of Mantua, who was known as the Mantuan, wrote the highly regarded *Eclogues*.

Holofernes continued, "Ah, good old Mantuan! I may speak of thee as the traveller doth of Venice: *Venetia, Venetia, chi non ti vede non ti pretia.*"

The Italian words mean, "Venice, Venice, he who does not see you does not value you."

In other words, anyone who sees Venice loves Venice.

Holofernes continued, "Old Mantuan, old Mantuan! Who understandeth thee not, loves thee not."

He began to sing a musical scale of notes: "*Ut, re, sol, la, mi, fa.*"

Later, "do" replaced "ut."

Holofernes had sung the scale of notes in the wrong order. This is the right order: *ut (do), re, mi, fa, sol, la.*

He then asked Sir Nathaniel, "Under pardon, sir, what are the contents of the letter? Or rather, as Horace says in his —"

While talking, he glanced at the letter, and surprised by what he saw, he said, "— what, on my soul, verses?"

Sir Nathaniel replied, "Aye, sir, and the verses are very learned."

Holofernes requested, "Let me hear a staff, a stanze, a verse; *lege, domine.*"

"*Lege, domine*" is Latin for "Read, sir."

Sir Nathaniel read the verses, which formed a sonnet:

"*If love make me forsworn, how shall I swear to love?*"

The sonnet, of course, was written by Biron, who wanted Rosaline to read it. This line means, "If falling in love makes me break my oath not to fall in love, how then can I swear an oath that I am in love?"

"*Ah, never faith could hold, if not to beauty vow'd!*

"*Though to myself forsworn, to thee I'll faithful prove.*

"*Those thoughts to me were oaks, to thee like osiers bowed.*"

In other words, when I swore my oath, I thought that it would stand as firmly as an oak and not bow before anything, but when I saw you the words of my oath became flexible like willow branches and bowed before you.

Osiers are willows.

"*Study his bias leaves and makes his book thine eyes,*"

In other words, seeing you, the student sets aside his favorite subject to study and instead studies your eyes.

"*Where all those pleasures live that art would comprehend.*

"*If knowledge be the mark, to know thee shall suffice;*

"*Well learned is that tongue that well can thee commend,*

"*All ignorant that soul that sees thee without wonder;*

"*Which is to me some praise that I thy parts admire.*"

Biron meant that he deserved some praise for being intelligent enough to admire the personal characteristics of Rosaline.

"*Thy eye Jove's lightning bears, thy voice his dreadful thunder,*"

Jove is Jupiter, King of the gods.

"*Which not to anger bent, is music and sweet fire.*"

"Not to anger bent" meant "not angry."

"*Celestial as thou art, oh, pardon, love, this wrong,*

"*That sings Heaven's praise with such an Earthly tongue.*"

Holofernes complained about Sir Nathaniel's reading, "You find not the *apostrophas*, and so miss the accent."

The apostrophe is used to indicate a missing vowel, and so it is used in contractions and to show other elisions — two syllables become one syllable when they are elided. If poetry contains elisions, and the elisions are not properly pronounced, words can be accented incorrectly and the meter thrown off.

But did Holofernes know what he was saying? Biron's sonnet contains one contraction — *vow'd* — of a word that is sometimes pronounced as two syllables in poetry. Were any other elisions needed?

Holofernes said, "Let me supervise the *canzonet*."

In other words, let me look over the little poem.

He continued, "Here are only numbers ratified; but, as for the elegancy, facility, and golden cadence of poesy, *caret*."

"Numbers ratified" are "verses that are metrically correct" — the verses have the correct stresses and number of syllables.

"*Caret*" is Latin for "it is lacking."

Holofernes continued with praise for Ovid, author of the *Metamorphoses*. Ovid's family name is "Naso," which means "nose."

He said, "Ovidius Naso was the man, and why, indeed, Naso, but for smelling out the odoriferous flowers of fancy, the jerks of invention?"

The "jerks of invention" are "flashes of inspiration." Holofernes was praising Ovid for his inspiration, and he went on to accuse Biron of being a mere imitator — someone who followed someone else.

The Latin word "*imitari*" means "to imitate."

Holofernes said, "*Imitari* is nothing: so doth the hound his master, the ape his keeper, the tired horse his rider."

To imitate someone is to be led by his example. The dog and the ape can be led by leashes tied to their necks, and a tired horse can be led by the reins. The dog, the ape, and the tired horse follow whichever man leads them by the leash or the rein.

He then said to Jaquenetta, "But, *damosella* virgin, was this directed to you?"

"*Damosella*" means "damsel" or "maiden." It is Medieval Latin.

Jaquenetta replied, "Aye, sir, from one Monsieur Biron, one of the strange Queen's lords."

The word "strange" meant "foreign."

Previously, Jaquenetta had said that Armado had sent the poem to her. Perhaps she realized that Armado was incapable of writing in this style, and perhaps she had learned from Costard that Biron had written a letter and asked him to deliver it. Of course, she was wrong when she said that Biron was one of the strange Queen's — ahem, Princess' — lords; Biron was one of the King's lords.

Holofernes said, "I will overglance the superscript."

This meant, "I will look at to whom this is addressed."

He read out loud, "*To the snow-white hand of the most beauteous Lady Rosaline.*"

Rosaline was dark-skinned; "snow-white" was a conventional compliment in a society that valued light skin.

Holofernes then said, "I will look again on the intellect of the letter, for the nomination of the party writing to the person written unto."

The intellect of the letter was the person writing the letter — that person had used his intellect to write the letter. Holofernes wanted to find out that person's "nomination," which Holofernes misused for "name." "Nomination," however, does have a Latin root that means "name": *nomine*.

He read out loud, "*Your ladyship's in all desired employment, BIRON.*"

Biron was offering to do whatever Rosaline wanted him to do: "all desired employment."

Holofernes said, "Sir Nathaniel, this Biron is one of the votaries with the King; and here he has framed a letter to a sequent of the stranger Queen's, which accidentally, or by the way of progression, has miscarried."

A "sequent" is a "follower."

Holofernes was saying that the letter had been delivered to the wrong person, either accidentally or because of the route it had traveled.

He then said to Jaquenetta, "Trip and go, my sweet. Deliver this paper into the royal hand of the King: it may concern much and be important. Stay not thy compliment; I forgive thy duty; adieu."

Holofernes wanted Jaquenetta to hurry; she need not curtsy to him and take a formal leave-taking.

Jaquenetta said, "Good Costard, go with me."

She then said, "Sir, may God save your life!"

"Have with thee, my girl," Costard said. "I will go with you."

Costard and Jaquenetta exited.

Complimenting Holofernes on his decision to have Jaquenetta deliver the letter to King Ferdinand, Sir Nathaniel said, "Sir, you have done this in the fear of God, very religiously; and, as a certain Father saith —"

The Father was a Father of the Church.

Holofernes interrupted, "— tell me not of the father; I do fear colorable colors."

In the proverb "I fear no colors," the word "colors" means "battle flags." A now rare definition of "colorable" is "fraudulent." Therefore, "colorable colors" could mean "fraudulent battle flags." Apparently, Holofernes wanted to avoid religious disputation. Discussing religion can lead to battles, both metaphoric and physical. Holofernes may also have been thinking that the father was a Catholic priest. He wanted to avoid any disputes between Catholic and Protestant theology. Catholics could say that Protestants fought under a fraudulent battle flag, and vice versa.

Holofernes then said, "But to return to the verses: Did they please you, Sir Nathaniel?"

Sir Nathaniel replied, "I liked them marvelously well for the penmanship."

Holofernes said, "I dine today at the home of the father of a certain pupil of mine; where, if, before repast, it shall please you to gratify the table with a grace, I will, on my privilege I have with the parents of the foresaid child or pupil, undertake your *ben venuto*; where I will prove those verses to be very unlearned, neither savoring of poetry, wit, nor invention. I beseech your society."

"*Ben venuto*" is Italian for "welcome."

Sir Nathaniel said, "And I thank you, too; for society, saith the text, is the happiness of life."

Holofernes said, "And, *certes*, the text most infallibly concludes it."

"*Certes*" is French for "certainly."

Holofernes then said to Constable Dull, "Sir, I do invite you, too. You shall not say me nay: *pauca verba*."

"*Pauca verba*" is Latin for "few words." A proverb stated, "Few words are best."

Holofernes continued, "Away! Let's go! The gentlefolk are at their game, and we will go to our own recreation."

Biron stood alone, holding a paper, in King Ferdinand's park.

He said these things to himself:

"The King is hunting the deer; I am coursing — pursuing and hunting — myself."

A husband and wife become one. Biron, who was not married, was seeking his other, better half.

Biron continued to speak to himself: "They have pitched a toil, a net into which the game will be driven so that it can be shot; I am toiling in a pitch — I am trying to get out of the mess I am in."

He was thinking of Rosaline's pitch-black eyes — eyes that had captured him in a net of love and had caused him to break his oath to stay away from women. Literally, pitch is boiled-down tar, a deep-black substance.

Biron continued to speak to himself: "This is pitch that defiles."

He was thinking of this proverb: "He that touches pitch shall be defiled."

The proverb was derived from Ecclesiasticus 13:1, which is part of the Apocrypha: "*He that toucheth pitch, shal be defiled therewith, and hee that hath fellowship with a proude man, shall be like vnto him*" (1611 King James Version).

Biron continued to speak to himself: "Defile! A foul word.

"Well, set yourself down, sorrow, and stay awhile! In other words, I must have patience. For so they say the fool said, and so say I, and therefore I am also a fool. Well proven, wit! I am definitely a fool; my thoughts prove it!

"By the Lord, this love is as mad as Ajax: This love kills sheep. It kills me, and therefore I am a sheep. Well proven again on my side! My wit gets much credit for correct reasoning!"

During the Trojan War, Achilles, the greatest Greek warrior, was killed. Afterwards, his armor was awarded to one of the living Greeks. According to Quintus of Smyrna's epic poem *Posthomerica*, the armor was awarded to the Greek warrior who had done the most to recover the corpse of Achilles. Two warriors — Great Ajax and Odysseus — had done the most to recover Achilles' corpse, and so a vote was taken to determine which of the two would get the armor. Achilles' armor was awarded to Odysseus, and this hurt Great Ajax so much that he went insane. According to Sophocles' tragedy *Ajax*, Great Ajax slaughtered sheep, thinking that they were Odysseus and Agamemnon, the main leader of the Greeks against the Trojans.

Biron continued to speak to himself: "I will not love. If I do, hang me; truly and faithfully, I will not love.

"Oh, but her eye — by this light, but for her eye, I would not love her; yes, for her two eyes."

Biron had mentioned one eye, and then he had mentioned Rosaline's two eyes. The one eye could be her vagina.

Biron continued to speak to himself: "Well, I do nothing in the world but lie, and I lie in my throat."

"To lie in one's throat" is to be an outrageous liar.

Biron continued to speak to himself: "By Heaven, I do love, and it has taught me to rhyme as I write sonnets, and to be melancholy. Here in my hand is part of my rhyme, and here is my melancholy."

He was referring to the paper he was holding in his hands; on it he had written a sonnet.

Biron continued to speak to himself: "Well, she has one of my sonnets already. The clown — Costard — bore it, the fool — me — sent it, and the lady — Rosaline — has it: sweet clown, sweeter fool, sweetest lady!

"By the world, I would not care a pin, if the other three were in the same situation I am in."

In other words, Biron would not mind if King Ferdinand, Longaville, and Dumain were also in love.

Biron looked up, saw someone coming, and said to himself, "Here comes someone holding a piece of paper. May God give him grace to groan because he is in love!"

Biron climbed a tree.

King Ferdinand walked under the tree and said, "Ay me!"

"Ay me" is an expression indicating sorrow.

Biron said to himself, "Shot by immortal Cupid and in love, by Heaven! Proceed, sweet Cupid. You have thumped him with your bird-bolt under the left pap and in his heart. Truly, I will hear secrets!"

A bird-bolt is a blunt arrow used by mortals to shoot birds.

King Ferdinand read out loud the sonnet he had written:

"So sweet a kiss the golden Sun gives not

"To those fresh morning drops upon the rose,

"As thy eye-beams, when their fresh rays have smote

"The night of dew that on my cheeks down flows:"

The "night of dew" refers to the tears that the lovesick King Ferdinand sheds at night.

"Nor shines the silver Moon one half so bright

"Through the transparent bosom of the deep,"

The "deep" is the "night."

"As doth thy face through tears of mine give light;

"Thou shinest in every tear that I do weep:"

By "Thou shinest," King Ferdinand meant "Your reflection shines."

"No drop but as a coach doth carry thee;

"So ridest thou triumphing in my woe."

In the above two lines, King Ferdinand compared the Princess of France to a woman who had conquered him and now was riding a coach — a chariot — in a Roman triumphal procession.

"Do but behold the tears that swell in me,

"And they thy glory through my grief will show:

"But do not love thyself; then thou wilt keep

"My tears for glasses, and still make me weep."

The "glasses" are looking-glasses, aka mirrors.

"Oh, Queen of Queens! How far dost thou excel,

"No thought can think, nor tongue of mortal tell."

King Ferdinand then said to himself, "How shall she know my griefs? I'll drop this paper somewhere she can find it."

He saw someone coming and said, "Sweet leaves, shade — hide — my folly. Who is he who comes here?"

He hid behind the tree and said, "What, Longaville! And he is reading! Listen, my ears."

Biron said to himself, "Now, in your likeness, one more fool appears!"

Longaville, carrying pieces of paper stuck in his hat, said to himself, "Ay me, I am forsworn! I have broken my oath!"

Biron said, "Why, he comes in like a perjurer, wearing papers."

In this society, people who had perjured themselves were forced to display a sign on themselves that stated their offense.

King Ferdinand said to himself, "He is in love like me, I hope. We have a sweet fellowship in shame!"

Biron said to himself, "One drunkard loves another of the name."

Longaville asked himself, "Am I the first who has perjured himself so?"

Biron said, "I could give you comfort. Not by just two whom I know, for there is a third. You make up the triumvirate, the corner-cap of society, the shape of Love's Tyburn that hangs up simplicity and foolishness."

Biron had mentioned things that formed a three. A triumvirate is a political group composed of three men. A corner-cap is a cap that has three sides. At the village of Tyburn was a gallows made of three wooden beams.

Longaville said to himself, "I fear these stubborn lines lack the power to move my beloved emotionally."

He read out loud, "*Oh, sweet Maria, empress of my love!*"

Then he said to himself, "These verses I will tear up, and write in prose."

He tore up the sonnet.

Biron said to himself, "Oh, rhymes are guards on wanton Cupid's hose. Disfigure not his shop."

In this society, the hose — tights or trousers — that men wore contained a codpiece that covered and accentuated the genitals; often codpieces were highly decorated. "Guards" are "ornamental trimmings." "Cupid's shop" is where he does his work — the genitals.

Longaville looked at another piece of paper and said, "This poem shall go to my beloved."

He read his sonnet out loud:

"*Did not the Heavenly rhetoric of thine eye,*

"*'Gainst which the world cannot hold argument,*

"*Persuade my heart to this false perjury?*

"*Vows for thee broke deserve not punishment.*

"*A woman I forswore; but I will prove,*"

By "forswore," Longaville meant "renounced." By "prove," Longaville meant "establish to be true."

"*Thou being a goddess, I forswore not thee:*

"*My vow was Earthly, thou a Heavenly love;*

"*Thy grace being gained cures all disgrace in me.*

"*Vows are but breath, and breath a vapor is:*"

A proverb stated, "Words are but wind."

"Then thou, fair Sun, which on my Earth dost shine,

"Exhalest this vapor-vow; in thee it is:"

By "exhalest," Longaville meant "draw up" or "evaporate."

"If broken then, it is no fault of mine:

"If by me broke, what fool is not so wise

"To lose an oath to win a paradise?"

Biron said to himself, "This is the lover-vein, which makes flesh a deity, and which makes a green goose — an immature girl — a goddess: It is pure, pure idolatry. God amend us, God amend us! We are much out of the way. May God help us! We lovers are far gone."

Longaville asked himself, "By whom shall I send this sonnet to Maria?"

He looked up, saw someone coming, and said to himself, "Company! Wait!"

He hid himself.

Biron said to himself, "All hid, all hid — just like in the old game Hide-and-Seek that is played by children. Like a demigod here sit I in the sky, and wretched fools' secrets heedfully overeye."

Seeing Dumain arriving and carrying a piece of paper, he added, "More sacks to the mill! Oh, Heavens, I have my wish! All of us are in love! Dumain is transformed into a lover! We are four woodcocks in the same dish!"

Woodcocks are proverbially stupid birds.

Dumain said to himself, "Oh, most divine Kate!"

Biron, whose opinion of Katherine was different, said to himself, "Oh, most profane coxcomb!"

A coxcomb was a hat worn by a professional jester; it resembled the comb of a cock, aka rooster. In other words, Biron was saying that she had the head of a fool.

Dumain said to himself, "By Heaven, the wonder in a mortal eye!"

Biron said to himself, "By Earth, she is not a wonder. Corporal — there you lie."

Dumain was a Corporal in the army of Love.

Dumain said to himself, "Her amber hair for foul has amber quoted."

He meant that the amber of Katherine's hair makes real amber seem ugly. People see her amber hair and declare that real amber is ugly.

Actually, Dumain's words were ambiguous. They could also be interpreted as saying this: Real amber makes the amber of Katherine's hair seem ugly. People see real amber and declare that Katherine's amber hair is ugly.

Biron said to himself, "An amber-colored raven was well noted."

In other words, it would be notable to find an amber-colored raven. By saying this, Biron was also comparing Katherine to a raven; in other words, she was ugly. The raven was regarded as a foul fowl.

Dumain said to himself, "She is as upright as the cedar."

Biron said to himself, "Stoop, I say; get your head out of the clouds. She has a rounded shoulder — it looks as if her shoulder is pregnant with a child."

Dumain said to himself, "She is as fair as day."

Biron said to himself, "Yes, she is as fair as some days — the days during which the Sun doesn't shine."

Dumain said to himself, "Oh, that I had my wish!"

Longaville said to himself, "And that I had mine!"

King Ferdinand said to himself, "And I mine, too, good Lord!"

Biron said to himself, "Amen, as long as I had mine. Isn't 'mine' a good word?"

Dumain said to himself, "I would forget her, but like a fever she reigns in my blood and she will be remembered."

Biron said to himself, "A fever in your blood! Why, then incision would let her out in saucers. Sweet misprision! Sweet deficient comparison!"

In this society, fevers were often treated by bloodletting. A shallow incision was made so the patient would bleed, and the blood was collected in saucers.

Dumain said to himself, "Once more I'll read the ode that I have written."

Biron said to himself, "Once more I'll mark how love can vary wit — how love can change an intelligent man's thinking and cause him to express that love in different ways."

Dumain read his poem out loud:

"On a day — alack the day! —

"Love, whose month is ever May,

"Spied a blossom passing fair"

The word "passing" meant "surpassingly."

"Playing in the wanton air:

"Through the velvet leaves the wind,

"All unseen, can passage find;"
The word "can" — an archaic verb — meant "did."
"That the lover, sick to death,"
The word "That" meant "So that."
"Wished himself the Heaven's breath.
"'Air,' quoth he, 'thy cheeks may blow;
"'Air,' quoth he, 'thy cheeks may blow;
"'Air, would I might triumph so!
"'But, alack, my hand is sworn
"'Never to pluck thee from thy thorn;
"'Vow, alack, for youth unmeet,'"
The word "unmeet" meant "unsuitable" and "improper."
"'Youth so apt to pluck a sweet!
"'Do not call it sin in me,
"'That I am forsworn for thee;
"'Thou for whom Jove would swear
"'Juno but an Ethiope were;
"'And deny himself for Jove,
"'Turning mortal for thy love.'"
"'Turning mortal for thy love.'"

The last four lines stated that Jove, aka Jupiter, King of the gods, would, for love of Katherine, say that his wife, Juno, was as ugly as an Ethiopian — most people in this society thought that Ethiopians were ugly because most people in this society valued light hair and light skin. Jove would also give up his immortality and his position as King of the gods so that he could be with Katherine.

Dumain said to himself, "This poem I will send to Katherine, and something else more plain that shall express my true love's fasting pain. My love is fasting because it is unrequited.

"Oh, I wish that the King, Biron, and Longaville were lovers, too, like me! Ill, to example ill, would from my forehead wipe a perjured note; for none offend where all alike do dote."

In other words, one lovesick man, to help another lovesick man, would from his forehead wipe away a mark of perjury. One way to do this would be for all men who had sworn not to love to break their vows by loving. When everyone breaks a vow, no one points out that someone has broken the vow.

In this society, people who had perjured themselves were forced to display a sign on themselves that stated their offense. Dumain was referring to that kind of sign.

In addition, he was referring to a love sonnet that a lovesick man such as himself or Longaville could stick in his hat. The love sonnet expressed a true love, but it was a perjured note because its existence showed that the author had broken a vow not to pursue a woman.

In addition, in Dante's *Purgatory*, an angel marks seven P's on the foreheads of saved sinners beginning to climb the Mountain of Purgatory in order to purge themselves of the seven deadly sins. As each of the seven levels of the mountain is climbed, one of the seven deadly sins is purged and an angel uses a wing to remove one of the P's from the sinner's forehead.

When Dumain said that "for none offend where all alike do dote," he meant that if each of the four men — himself, King Ferdinand, Biron, and Longaville — committed perjury by breaking their oath, none of them would blame the others because they had all broken the same oath. This is true — once every man's lovesickness has been revealed.

Longaville came out of hiding and said, "Dumain, your love is far from Christian charity. You may look pale, but I also would blush, I know, if I were overheard and taken napping so."

King Ferdinand came out of hiding and said to Longaville, "Come, sir, you blush. As his is, your case is also such. You chide him, although you offend twice as much.

"You do not love Maria? Longaville did never a sonnet for her sake write, nor ever lay his wreathed, folded arms athwart his loving bosom to keep down his heart?"

The heart of a lovesick or otherwise emotionally excited man can beat rapidly. In this society, people would thump their chest to keep their heart from beating so rapidly. In this case, Longaville could simply fold his arms over his chest — a position a lover often takes — and that would keep his heart from beating so rapidly.

King Ferdinand continued, "I have been closely shrouded in this bush and watched you both and saw that you both blushed. I heard your guilty rhymes, observed your fashion of acting, saw sighs exude from you, and noted well your passion: 'Ay me!' says one. 'Oh, Jove!' the other cries.

"One says her hairs are gold; the other says crystal are the other beloved's eyes.

"You, Longaville, would for paradise break faith, and your oath.

"And Dumain, if you were Jove, for your love you would infringe an oath.

"What will Biron say when he shall hear that your oath and faith are so infringed, which with such zeal you did swear? How he will scorn! How he will expend his wit! How he will triumph, leap with glee, and laugh at it!

"For all the wealth that ever I did see, I would not have him know so much about me."

Biron said to himself, "Now I will step forth and whip hypocrisy."

He climbed out of the tree and said, "Ah, my good liege, I pray that you pardon me! Good heart, what grace have you, thus to reprove these worms for loving, when you are the most in love?

"Your eyes make no coaches? In your tears there is no certain Princess who appears? You'll not be perjured because it is a hateful thing?

"Tush, you say, none but minstrels like the act of sonneting!

"But aren't you ashamed? Aren't you, all three of you, ashamed to be thus much overshot? All of you said an oath and made study your target, but all of you missed that target.

"Longaville found Dumain's mote, the King did Longaville's mote see, but I a beam do find in the eye of each of you three."

A mote is a speck.

Biron was referring to Matthew 7:3: "*And why beholdest thou the mote that is in thy brother's eye, but considerest not the beam that is in thine own eye?*" (King James Bible).

Biron continued, "Oh, what a scene of foolery have I seen, of sighs, of groans, of sorrow, and of woeful teen! Oh, me, with what strict patience have I sat, to see a King transformed to a gnat! To see great Hercules whipping a gig, and profound Solomon tune a jig, and Nestor play at push-pin with the boys, and critic Timon laugh at idle toys and useless trivialities!"

Children sometimes played a game with a spinning top, aka gig. They would start it spinning, and then hit it with a whip to keep it spinning. To "tune a jig" is to sing or play a song. Push-pin was a game in which children tried to get pins into the other child's territory. Timon was a famous misanthrope whom William Shakespeare wrote about in his tragedy *Timon of Athens*.

Biron continued, "Where lies your grief, oh, tell me, good Dumain?

"And gentle Longaville, where lies your pain?

"And where lies my liege's?

"Your pains lie all about the breast. Someone bring a caudle, ho! Someone bring a medicinal drink!"

King Ferdinand said, "Too bitter is your jesting. Are we betrayed — exposed — thus to your over-view?"

"You are not betrayed by me, for I am betrayed by you," Biron said. "I, who am honest and who holds it to be a sin to break the vow that I am engaged in, am betrayed by keeping company with men like you — men of inconstancy.

"When shall you see me write a thing in rhyme? Or groan for Joan? Or spend a minute's time in preening myself? When shall you hear that I will praise a hand, a foot, a face, an eye, a walking gait, a posture, a brow, a breast, a waist, a leg, a limb?"

Biron, seeing Jaquenetta and Costard walking towards them, started to hurry away. He had given Costard a sonnet to give to Rosaline, and he feared that he would be first exposed as a lover and then exposed to ridicule.

"Wait!" King Ferdinand said. "Why are you hurrying away so fast? Is he a true man or a thief who gallops so?"

"I run posthaste away from love," Biron said. "Good lover, let me go."

Jaquenetta and Costard walked over to the men.

Jaquenetta said, "God bless the King!"

Seeing the letter Jaquenetta was holding, King Ferdinand asked, "What present have you there?"

Costard replied, "Some certain treason."

King Ferdinand asked, "What is treason making — doing — here?"

Costard said, "Treason makes nothing, sir."

King Ferdinand said, "If it mars nothing either, then the treason and you two may go away in peace together."

"I beseech your grace, let this letter be read," Jaquenetta said to the King as she handed him the letter. "Our person suspects it; it is treason, he said."

As she had done previously, Jaquenetta pronounced "parson" as "person." She was also mistaken about the person who suspected the letter; that person was the schoolmaster Holofernes, not the parson Sir Nathaniel. In addition, nothing at the time had been said about treason.

Handing Biron the letter, King Ferdinand said, "Biron, read it over."

He then asked Jaquenetta, "Where did you get the letter?"

"From Costard."

King Ferdinand asked Costard, "Where did you get it?"

"From Dun Adramadio, Dun Adramadio."

Of course, he meant Don Armado.

Biron recognized his own handwriting, and he tore up the letter.

"What are you doing?" King Ferdinand asked. "What is the matter with you? Why did you tear up the letter?"

Biron replied, "It is a trifling thing like a toy, my liege, just a toy. Your grace needs not fear it."

Longaville said, "It caused Biron to feel strong emotion, and therefore let's hear it."

Dumain gathered up the pieces from the ground, looked at them, and said, "This is Biron's handwriting, and here is his name."

Biron said to Costard, "Ah, you useless blockhead! You were born to do me shame."

He then said to King Ferdinand, "I am guilty, my lord, guilty! I confess, I confess."

"You confess what?" King Ferdinand asked.

"I confess that you three fools lacked me — a fourth fool — to make up the mess of four who dine together at a table. He, he, and you — that's you, my liege — and I are pick-purses in love, we are trying to steal love, and we deserve to die."

In this society, the usual punishment for pick-purses — that is, pickpockets — was death by hanging.

Biron continued, "Oh, dismiss this audience, and I shall tell you more."

"Now the number is even," Dumain said.

The goose — Biron — made the number even. He was the *l'envoi*.

"True, true; we are four," Biron said. "Will these turtledoves — these lovers, Jaquenetta and Costard — be gone?"

King Ferdinand said to Jaquenetta and Costard. "Hence, sirs; away!"

In this society, the word "sir" could be used to refer to a woman.

Costard said, "The true — loyal — folk now walk away, and they let the traitors stay."

Costard and Jaquenetta walked away.

Biron said, "Sweet lords, sweet lovers — oh, let us embrace! We are as true — steadfast — as flesh and blood can be. We are true to our youth and the reason we were born. The sea will ebb and flow, Heaven will show its face; young blood does not obey an old decree, and we cannot cross, aka oppose, the cause, aka reason, why we were born."

Young hot-blooded men do not obey an old decree. Even if they swear an oath to take up study and give up women, they are unable to keep that oath.

Young hot-blooded men also cannot oppose the reason why they were born — they cannot oppose their lustful feelings. We are born to have children and perpetuate the human species.

Biron continued, "Therefore, all of us must be forsworn. All of must break our oath."

King Ferdinand asked, "Did these torn-up lines of writing reveal some love of yours?"

"Did they, ask you?" Biron replied. "Whoever sees the Heavenly Rosaline will act like an uncivilized and savage Sun-worshipping man of India, seeing the first dawning of the gorgeous east. Both will bow their vassal head and, having been struck blind, either by the Sun or by the beauty of Rosaline, both will touch the base ground with obedient breast.

"What peremptory eagle-sighted eye that dares look upon the Heaven of Rosaline's brow will not be blinded by her majesty?"

Eagles were reputed to be able to stare at the Sun without harming their eyes, but according to Biron, the beauty of Rosaline would blind even a person with eyes like those of an eagle.

King Ferdinand said, "What zeal, what fury, has inspired you now? My love, the Princess, who is Rosaline's superior, is a gracious Moon. Compared to my love, Rosaline is an attending star, a scarcely seen light."

Biron replied, "My eyes are then no eyes, nor am I Biron. Oh, but for my love, day would turn to night! Of all complexions the culled sovereignty — the excellence selected as the highest — meet, as at a fair, in her fair cheek, where several worthy beauties make one perfect beauty, where nothing is missing that the desire for perfection itself does seek.

"Lend me the flourish of all gentle tongues, the embellishment of all civilized languages — bah, that is painted, artificial, cosmetic rhetoric! Oh, Rosalind does not need it. To things for sale a seller's praise belongs; sellers praise what they have for sale, hoping that someone will buy from them. Rosaline surpasses praise, and therefore praise is inadequate to do her beauty justice and so praise becomes a blot and a blemish.

"A withered hermit, five-score winters worn, might shake off fifty of his hundred years, looking her in the eye. Looking at a beautiful woman varnishes and renews an aged man, making him as if he were newly born, and to the old man with the crutch it gives the infancy of a babe in the cradle.

"Oh, beauty is the Sun that makes all things shine."

King Ferdinand said, "By Heaven, your love is as black as ebony."

Biron said, "Is ebony like her? Oh, wood and word divine! A wife made of such wood would be felicity itself.

"Oh, who can help me to give an oath? Where is a Holy Bible so that I may swear beauty does beauty lack, if beauty does not learn from looking at Rosaline's face how beauty should look. No face is fair that is not fully as black as the face of Rosaline."

Biron was not only saying that black is beautiful; he was also saying that only black is beautiful.

"Oh, that is a paradox!" King Ferdinand said. "Black is the badge — the distinguishing sign — of Hell; it is the hue of dungeons and the suit of night. Beauty's true badge, which is lightness, becomes the Heavens well."

Biron replied, "Devils soonest tempt when they resemble spirits of light."

He was thinking of II Corinthians 11:14: "*And no marvel: for Satan himself is transformed into an Angel of light*" (1599 Geneva Bible).

Biron continued, "Oh, if in black my lady's forehead is decked, that black mourns that cosmetics and wigs should ravish doters with a false appearance, and therefore Rosaline was born to make black fair.

"Rosaline's appearance changes the fashion of these days, for native blood — rosiness — is thought to be devalued like cosmetics now, and therefore a woman with a naturally pink complexion who wants to avoid dispraise, uses cosmetics to make herself black in order to imitate Rosaline's black forehead."

Dumain said, "To look like Rosaline, chimney-sweepers make themselves black."

Longaville said, "And since Rosaline's beauty became fashionable, colliers are accounted bright."

A collier is a dealer in charcoal or pit-coal.

King Ferdinand said, "And Ethiopians boast about their sweet complexion."

Dumain said, "Dark needs no candles now, for dark is light."

Biron said, "Your lady friends never dare to come in contact with rain, for fear their colors — which are due to cosmetics — would be washed away."

King Ferdinand said, "It would be good, if yours did; for, sir, to tell you plain, I'll find a fairer face that has not washed today."

Biron replied, "I'll prove that Rosaline is fair, aka beautiful, or I'll talk until doomsday here."

King Ferdinand said, "No devil will frighten you then so much as she."

Dumain said, "I never before knew a man to hold such vile stuff so dear."

Longaville raised one of his feet, on which were black shoes, and said, "Look, here's your love. Look at my foot and see her face."

Biron said, "Oh, if the streets were paved with your eyes, her feet would be much too dainty for such a path to tread!"

"Oh, vile!" Dumain said, "Then, as she walks, what upward lies the street would see as she walked overhead. The street, if it had my eyes, would be able to look up her skirt."

"But what about all this?" King Ferdinand said. "Aren't we all in love?"

"Nothing is as sure as that we are all in love," Biron said, "and thereby we are all forsworn. All of us have broken our oath."

"Then let us stop this chattering," King Ferdinand said, "and, good Biron, now prove that our loving is lawful, and that our faith is not torn. Make a reasonable argument that our falling in love is allowed and that we have not actually broken our oath."

"Yes, indeed, do that!" Dumain said. "We need some clever trickery with words to show that we have not done this evil of perjury."

"Oh, we need some authority, some precedent, on how to proceed," Longaville said. "We need some tricks, some subtle distinctions, that will teach us how to cheat the devil."

"We need some salve for perjury," Dumain said.

Biron rose to the occasion.

"It is more than necessary," he said. "Here goes, then, affection's men at arms. All of us are now warriors in Love's army.

"Consider what you first did swear to do: to fast, to study, and to see no women. That is flat treason against the Kingly status of youth.

"Say, can you fast? Your stomachs are too young and inexperienced, and abstinence engenders maladies. Not eating causes illness.

"Oh, we have made a vow to study, lords, and in that vow we have forsworn our books. For when would you, my liege, or you, Longaville, or you, Dumain, in leaden and dull contemplation have learned to write such fiery, passionate verses as the prompting eyes of beauty's tutors have enriched you with?

"Other slow arts occupy the brain, and only the brain, and therefore scarcely show a harvest from the heavy toil of their barren and uninspired practitioners. These dreary studies occupy the brain and have no application outside of the brain.

"But love, first learned in a lady's eyes, lives not alone immured and walled up in the brain. Instead, love, with the speed of winds and storms, runs as swiftly as thought in every faculty and function, and gives to every faculty and function a double power, over and above their customary functions.

"Love adds a precious seeing to the eye. A lover's eyes will gaze an eagle blind. The eyes of a lover can look at an eagle and make the eagle blind, proving that the lover is brighter than the Sun, which cannot blind the eagle.

"A lover's ear will hear the lowest sound. When the ears of a thief, who is suspicious of every sound, are shut, the lover's ears will still be able to hear.

"Love's feeling is softer and more sensitive than are the tender horns of snails who carry around their shell.

"Love's tongue proves that dainty, fastidious Bacchus, the god of wine and feasting, is gross in taste in comparison.

"As for valor, is not Love a Hercules, constantly climbing trees in the garden of the Hesperides?"

One of Hercules' famous labors was stealing some golden apples from the garden of the Hesperides, immortal nymphs who lived in the west and took care of the garden.

Biron continued, "Love is as subtle as the Sphinx and as sweet and musical as bright Apollo's lute, which is strung with his hair."

The Sphinx is a mythological creature with the head of a human and the body of a lion. In Sophocles' tragedy *Oedipus Rex*, the Sphinx, which has the head of a woman, asks Oedipus this riddle: What goes on four legs in the morning, two legs at noon, and three legs in the evening? If Oedipus cannot answer this riddle correctly, the Sphinx will kill him. Fortunately, Oedipus does answer the riddle correctly: Man, who goes on hands and knees as a crawling baby, two legs as a healthy adult, and two legs and a cane as an old person.

Biron continued, "And when Love speaks, the voices of all the gods make Heaven drowsy with the harmony.

"Never has a poet dared to touch a pen to write until his ink is mixed with Love's sighs. Oh, once his pen is so mixed, then his lines ravish savage ears and plant mild humility in tyrants.

"From women's eyes I derive this doctrine. Women's eyes sparkle with the true Promethean fire — they constantly throw out sparks of the true Promethean fire."

Prometheus, who was a Titan (one of the primordial — which means existing from the beginning of time — giant gods who ruled the Earth until Zeus conquered them), stole fire from the gods and gave it to early Humankind. In some versions of the myth, the fire was the spark of life.

Biron continued, "Women's eyes are the books, the arts, the academies, that show, contain, and nourish all the world. Without the help of women's eyes, no man can prove to be excellent in anything.

"And you were fools to forswear these women, or if you keep the oath you swore, you will prove to be fools.

"For wisdom's sake, a word that all men love,

"Or for love's sake, a word that loves — inspires and is lovable to — all men,

"Or for men's sake, the authors of these women,

"Or for women's sake, by whom we men are men,

"Let us immediately and once and for all time lose our oaths so that we can find ourselves, or else we will lose ourselves by keeping our oaths."

Biron was thinking of Matthew 16:25: "*For whosoever will save his life shall lose it: and whosoever will lose his life for my sake shall find it*" (1599 Geneva Bible).

"It is within the beliefs of our religion to be thus forsworn, for charity itself fulfills the law, and who can sever love from charity?"

Biron was thinking of Romans 13:8: "*Owe nothing to any man, but to love one another; for he that loveth another, hath fulfilled the Law*" (1599 Geneva Bible).

One meaning of "Who can sever love from charity?" is "Who can separate *amor* (sexual love) from *caritas* (spiritual love)?"

Biron was thinking of 1 Corinthians 13:13: "*And now abideth faith, hope and love, even these three; but the chiefest of these is love*" (1599 Geneva Bible). In many translations, the word "charity" is used instead of "love." For example, this is the translation in the King James Bible: "*And now abideth faith, hope, charity, these three; but the greatest of these is charity.*"

King Ferdinand said, "Saint Cupid, then! And, soldiers, to the battlefield!"

"Saint Cupid" was a battle cry; the standard English battle cry was "Saint George!"

Biron said, "Advance your standards, and set upon them, lords. Pell-mell! Down with them! But be first advised that in our conflict you get the Sun of them."

This is one meaning of what Biron said: "Lift up the poles holding your battle flags and let's go fight the enemy. Pell-mell! Down with the enemy! But be first advised that in our conflict that you get the Sun so that it is shining in their faces; that will give us a military advantage."

This is another meaning of what Biron said: "Lift up the 'poles' in front and just under your waist and let's get on top of the ladies, lords. Fast and furious! Let's get active so that we can make the enemy 'die'! But be first advised that in our 'conflict' with the ladies we get each of them pregnant with a son."

In this society, one meaning of "die" is to "have an orgasm."

Longaville said, "Now to plain-dealing and plain-speaking; let us lay these glozes — bits of superficial wordplay — aside. Shall we resolve to woo these girls of France?"

"Yes, and to win them, too," King Ferdinand said. "Therefore, let us devise some entertainment for them in their tents."

Biron said, "First, from the park let us conduct the ladies toward that place, and as we head there let every man seize the hand of the fair woman he loves.

"In the afternoon we will with some exceptional pastime entertain them — some sort of entertainment that we can come up with in the short time we have to do the planning.

"We know that revels, dances, masquerades, and merry hours run before fair Love, strewing her way with flowers."

"Away! Away!" King Ferdinand said. "Let's go now! No time shall be omitted that will come to pass and may by us be fitted. We will make good use of all the time available to us."

Biron cried, "*Allons! Allons!*"

"*Allons! Allons!*" is French for "Let's go! Let's go!"

King Ferdinand, Longaville, and Dumain exited.

Alone, Biron said to himself, "Sowed cockle reaped no corn."

This means, "If you sow weeds, you will not reap wheat."

Biron continued, "And justice always whirls in equal measure: Light wenches may prove to be plagues to men forsworn. If so, our copper buys no better treasure."

This means, "Justice always whirls around like the Wheel of Fortune in a fair and equitable manner. Wanton women may prove to be plagues to men who have broken their vows. But even if so, our copper coins — which have little value — can buy no better treasure."

CHAPTER 5

— 5.1 —

The schoolmaster Holofernes, the curate Sir Nathaniel, and Constable Dull talked together in King Ferdinand's park. The three men had dined together at the home of the father of one of Holofernes' pupils.

Holofernes said, "*Satis quod sufficit.*"

The Latin sentence means, "Enough is sufficient." As a proverb, its meaning is this: "Enough is as good as a feast."

"I praise God for you, sir," Sir Nathaniel said to Holofernes. "Your remarks at dinner have been sharp and full of wise sayings; pleasant without scurrility, witty without affectation, audacious without impudence, learned without arrogance, and novel without heresy. I did converse the other day with a companion of the King's, who is graced with the name of, nominated, or called Don Adriano de Armado."

Holofernes said, "*Novi hominem tanquam te.*"

The Latin sentence means, "I know the man as well as I know you."

Holofernes continued, "Armado's disposition is lofty, his discourse peremptory and resolved, his tongue refined and smooth, his eye ambitious, his gait majestical, and his general behavior vain, ridiculous, and thrasonical — boastful and vainglorious. He is too picked, too spruce, too affected and foppish, too odd, as it were, too peregrinate and affectedly foreign, as I may call it."

Sir Nathaniel said, "A most singular and choice epithet — a most singular and appropriate turn of phrase."

He drew out his notebook so he could write down the phrase.

Holofernes said, "Armado draweth out the thread of his verbosity finer than the staple, aka material, of his argument, aka subject. I abhor such fanatical phantasimes."

A phantasime is an extravagantly behaved person.

Holofernes continued, "I abhor such insociable, aka intolerable, and point-devise, aka affectedly precise and immaculate, companions.

"I abhore such rackers of orthography — he is a person who tortures correct spelling, as we can tell by the way he pronounces words.

"Armado speaks 'dout,' *sine* b, when he should say 'doubt'; he speaks 'det,' when he should pronounce 'debt' — d, e, b, t, not d, e, t."

Sine is Latin for "without."

Holofernes continued, "Armado clepeth a calf, cauf; half, hauf; neighbor *vocatur* nebor; neigh abbreviated ne."

"Clepeth" is an archaic verb meaning "calls."

Holofernes pronounced the "igh" in the words "neighbor" and "neigh"; he pronounced it somewhat like one of the ways of pronouncing the German word "*ich*," which means "I."

"*Vocatur*" is a Latin word that means "is called."

Holofernes was a member of an English Renaissance group who wanted English words to be spelled and pronounced as closely as possible to those Latin words on which the English word was thought to be based. The English word "doute" became "doubt" because of the Latin word "*dubitum*," and the English word "dette" became "debt" because of the Latin word "*debitum*." Holofernes wanted the letter "b" in these words to be pronounced.

Holofernes continued, "This is abhominable — which he would call abominable."

People used to think that the word "abominable" came from the Latin phrase "*ab homine*," which means "away from man," or "unnatural." Actually, it comes from the Latin word "*abominabilis*," which means "contemptible."

Holofernes continued, "It insinuateth me of insanie. *Ne intelligis, domine*? To make frantic, lunatic."

Holofernes was complaining that such pronunciations drove him insane.

"*Ne intelligis, domine*?" is Latin for "Do you understand, sir?"

Sir Nathaniel said, "*Laus Deo, bone intelligo*."

He had meant to say, "Praise be to God, I understand well," but he made a mistake. He said "*bone*" instead of "*bene*."

Holofernes said, "*Bone*? *Bone* for *bene*? Priscian is a little scratched, but it will serve."

Priscian, who flourished in 500 A.D., was a scholar whose Latin grammar book was used for many centuries.

"To break Priscian's head" meant "to mangle Latin grammar." Here, Holofernes was saying that Sir Nathaniel's Latin was a little wrong, but it would serve — Holofernes understood what Sir Nathaniel meant.

Sir Nathaniel looked up and asked, "*Videsne quis venit?*"

The Latin sentence means, "Do you see who is coming?"

Holofernes looked and then replied, "*Video, et gaudeo.*"

The Latin sentence means, "I see, and I rejoice."

Don Adriana de Armado, Mote, and Costard walked over to Holofernes and Sir Nathaniel.

Armado greeted them: "Chirrah!"

As usual, Holofernes disliked Armado's pronunciation: "*Quare* 'chirrah,' not 'sirrah'?"

"*Quare* is Latin for "why."

"Sirrah" was a word used to address a male of inferior status to that of the speaker.

Armado said, "Men of peace, well encountered."

Holofernes replied, "Most military sir, salutation."

Mote said quietly to Costard, "They have been at a great feast of languages, and stolen the scraps."

Costard replied, "Oh, they have lived long on the alms-basket of words."

An alms-basket was a basket used to collect scraps of leftover food for the impoverished. Armado, Holofernes, and Sir Nathaniel used fancy words — those left over from the conversation of ordinary people, who do not use them.

Costard continued, "I marvel that your master has not eaten you for a word, for you are not so long by the head — as tall — as the word '*honorificabilitudinitatibus.*'"

"*Honorificabilitudinitatibus*" is the dative or ablative case of a Medieval Latin word that means, "In the state of being honored." The English word "honorificabilitudinity," meaning "honorableness," is interesting because it has only alternating vowels and consonants. The word appeared in *Bailey's Dictionary*, published in 1721.

Costard continued to remark on Mote's small size: "You are more easily swallowed than a flap-dragon."

A flap-dragon is a raisin in brandy that has been set on fire.

Mote said, "Peace! Silence! The peal begins."

The peal was the noise of conversation between Holofernes and Armado.

Armado asked Holofernes, "Monsieur, are you not lettered?"

Mote said, "Yes, yes, he is; he teaches boys the hornbook."

The hornbook was used in teaching. A leaf of paper showed the alphabet; it was placed on a wooden rectangular block with a handle and covered with transparent horn to protect it. When heated, horn becomes malleable. When scraped thin enough, horn is transparent.

Mote asked Holofernes, "What is 'a, b,' spelt backward, with the horn on his head?"

Holofernes replied, "The answer is 'ba,' *pueritia*, with a horn added."

The word "*pueritia*" is Latin for childhood; Holofernes was calling Mote a child.

Mote said, "Baa, most silly sheep with a horn. You hear his learning."

He was making fun of Holofernes by calling him a sheep.

Holofernes asked, "*Quis, quis*, you consonant?"

"*Quis*" is Latin for "who." He was asking, "Who is the sheep, consonant?"

By calling Mote a consonant, Holofernes was saying that Mote is insignificant. A vowel can form a syllable by itself, but a consonant cannot. To say "b," one must say the consonant "b" and the vowel "e."

Mote replied to Holofernes' question, "The third of the five vowels, if you repeat them; or the fifth, if I repeat them."

Holofernes said, "I will repeat them — a, e, i — "

Mote finished the sentence that began with Holofernes' "I": "— the sheep."

In other words, "I — that is, Holofernes — am the sheep."

Mote continued, "The other two vowels conclude it — o, u."

In other words, "Oh, ewe" or "Oh, you." "U" being the fifth of five syllables, as Mote pronounced them, "u" — that is, ewe, or you, Holofernes — is the sheep.

Armado, who got the joke, said, "Now, by the salt wave of the Mediterraneum, a sweet touch, a quick venue of wit! Snip, snap, quick and home! It rejoiceth my intellect: true wit!"

"Mediterraneum" was Armado's way of pronouncing "Mediterranean."

A "touch" is a "hit" in fencing; a "venue" is a "sword-thrust" in fencing. "Home" means "right to the target."

"To snip-snap" is "to engage in smart repartee." "Quick and home" means "by being quick, you hit the target."

Mote said, "Offered by a child to an old man, who is wit-old."

A "wittold" is a witting — knowing — cuckold, the husband who knows that he has an unfaithful wife but who does nothing about it.

Holofernes asked, "What is the figure? What is the figure?"

"Figure" means "figure of speech" or "emblem."

Mote replied, "Horns."

Horns were said to grow on the forehead of a cuckold, and so they were the emblems of a cuckold.

Holofernes said, "Thou disputest like an infant, a child. Go, whip thy gig."

"Whip thy gig" meant "play with your top." A whip could be used to keep a top spinning.

Mote said, "Lend me your horn to make one, and I will whip about your infamy *manu cita* — I will make a gig out of a cuckold's horn."

"*Manu cita*" is Latin for "with a ready hand."

Costard said to Mote, "If I had but just one penny in the world, I would give it to you so you can buy gingerbread. Wait, there is the very remuneration I had from your boss, you halfpenny — little — purse of wit, you pigeon-egg — small egg — of discretion."

Costard gave Mote some money and said, "Oh, if the Heavens were so pleased that they would make you my bastard, what a joyful father you would make me!

"There; you have it — the money — *ad* dunghill, at the fingers' ends, as they say."

A pile of manure is a dunghill; dung is manure.

Holofernes said, "Oh, I smell false Latin; Costard used 'dunghill' for 'unguem.'"

The word "*unguem*" is Latin for "fingertip." The Latin phrase "*ad unguem*" is Latin for "to the fingertip," which is idiomatic for "exact in detail."

Armado said to Holofernes, "Arts-man, aka scholar, preambulate, aka walk ahead of the others with me, we will be singuled, aka singled-out, from the barbarous. Do you not educate youth at the charge-house, aka school, on the top of the mountain?"

Holofernes replied, "Or *mons* — the hill."

Armado said, "At your sweet pleasure, for the mountain."

He preferred the more grandiose geographical structure.

Hearing "mounting," as in "sexual mounting," rather than "mountain," Holofernes replied, "I do, *sans* question."

"*Sans*" is French for "without."

Armado said, "Sir, it is the King's most sweet pleasure and affection to congratulate — salute — the Princess at her pavilion in the posteriors of this day, which the rude multitude call the afternoon."

"Posteriors" meant "later parts," as well as "buttocks."

Holofernes replied, "The posterior of the day, most generous and noble-minded sir, is liable and apt, congruent and fitting, and measurable and suited for the afternoon. The word is well culled, chosen, sweet, and apt, I do assure you, sir, I do assure you."

Armado replied, "Sir, the King is a noble gentleman, and my familiar, I do assure ye, my very good friend. As for what is inward and secret and private between us, let it pass. I do beseech and ask thee to remember thy courtesy. I beseech thee, apparel thy head."

The phrase "remember thy courtesy" means either "take your hat off" or "put your hat on."

Holofernes had taken off his hat for some reason.

Armado continued, "And among these private things the King and I have shared other importunate, burdensome, and most serious designs, and of great import indeed, too, but let that pass, for I must tell thee, it will please his grace, by the world, sometime to lean upon my poor shoulder, and with his royal finger, thus, dally with my excrescence, aka my hair, with my mustachio; but, sweet heart, let that pass.

"By the world, I recount no fable. Some certain special honors it pleaseth his greatness to impart to Armado, a soldier, a man of travel, who has seen the world; but let that pass.

"The very all of all, aka sum of everything, aka most important thing, is — but, sweet heart, I do implore secrecy — that the King would have me present the Princess, sweet chuck, aka sweet chick, with some delightful ostentation, or show, or pageant, or antic, aka grotesque show, or firework.

"Now, understanding that the curate and your sweet self are good at such eruptions of wit and sudden breakings out of mirth, as it were, I have acquainted you withal, to the end to crave your assistance."

Holofernes knew immediately the kind of entertainment that he wanted King Ferdinand — and Armado — to present to the Princess of France: "Sir, you shall present before her the Nine Worthies."

The Nine Worthies were nine great men: three from the Bible, three from classical times, and three from romances.

The three from the Bible were Joshua, King David, and Judas Maccabaeus.

The three from classical times were Hector of Troy, Alexander the Great, and Julius Caesar.

The three from romances were King Arthur, Holy Roman Emperor Charlemagne, and Godfrey of Bouillon.

Holofernes, however, wanted the Roman Pompey the Great and the mythological hero Hercules to be among the Nine Worthies.

Holofernes continued, "Sir, you shall present before her the Nine Worthies. Sir Nathaniel, as concerning some entertainment of time, some show in the posterior of this day, to be rendered by our assistants, at the King's command, and this most gallant, illustrate, and learned gentleman, before the Princess — I say none so fit as to present the Nine Worthies."

Holofernes was excited. He said "illustrate" instead of "illustrious," and his syntax was not clear. But it was clear that he wanted to present the Nine Worthies, and he believed that they could find performers who would be fit to present the Nine Worthies.

Sir Nathaniel asked, "Where will you find men worthy enough to present them?"

Holofernes replied, "Joshua, yourself; myself; and this gallant gentleman, Judas Maccabaeus."

Holofernes was so excited that he continued to not be clear. Perhaps he meant that he would play King David. "This gallant gentleman" was Armado.

He continued, "This swain, Costard, because of his great limb or joint and his great size, shall pass as Pompey the Great. The page, Mote, will be Hercules —"

Armado interrupted, "Pardon, sir; error. Mote is little; he is not quantity enough for that Worthy's thumb. Mote is not even as big as the end of Hercules' club."

"Shall I have audience?" Holofernes said. "Listen to me. Mote shall present Hercules in minority. He will play Hercules as a baby. His entrance and exit shall be strangling a snake; and I will have an apology — a prologue — for that purpose."

When Hercules was an infant, Juno, Queen of the gods, who hated Hercules because her husband, Jupiter, had cheated on her and fathered Hercules with a mortal woman, sent two snakes to kill him as he slept. The infant Hercules woke up and used his great strength to strangle the two snakes.

Mote said, "An excellent device! An excellent plan! So, if any of the audience hiss, you may cry, 'Well done, Hercules! Now you are crushing the snake!' That is the way to make an offense gracious, although few have the grace to do it."

Audiences hiss actors when audience members dislike them. But in this case, Holofernes could pretend that the hissing of the audience was the hissing of the snake.

Armado asked, "What about the rest of the Worthies?"

Holofernes replied, "I will play three myself."

Mote said, "You are a thrice-worthy gentleman!"

Armado asked, "Shall I tell you a thing?"

Holofernes replied, "We attend. We are listening."

Armado said, "We will have, if this fadge not, an antic."

In other words, "If this presentation of the Nine Worthies does not succeed, we will have an antic — a grotesque spectacle."

This could mean that if the presentation of the Nine Worthies failed, it would be a grotesque spectacle, or that if the presentation of the Nine Worthies failed, they would have as a backup entertainment an antic.

He then said, "I beseech you, follow me."

They had stopped to talk because Holofernes was so excited, but now Armado wanted to start walking again.

Holofernes said, "*Via*, goodman Dull!"

One meaning of "*Via*" in Italian is "Hurry up!"

He then said to Constable Dull, "Thou hast spoken no word all this while."

Constable Dull replied, "Nor understood none neither, sir."

"*Allons*!" Holofernes said. "We will employ thee. We will find something for thee to do."

"*Allons*!" is French for "Let's go!"

Constable Dull said, "I'll make one in a dance, or something like that; or I will play on the tabor — a small drum — to the Worthies, and let them dance the hay."

"Most dull, honest Dull!" Holofernes said. "To our sport, away! To our entertainment, let's go!"

The Princess, Rosaline, Maria, and Katherine talked together. They had received presents and poems from the men of Navarre who loved them: King Ferdinand, Biron, Longaville, and Dumain.

The Princess said, "Sweet hearts, we shall be rich before we depart Navarre and go home to France, if fairings come thus plentifully in."

"Fairings" are presents that are called "fairings" because the word originally referred to small presents bought at fairs.

The Princess, who had received a pendant depicting a lady with a border made of diamonds, said, "A lady walled about with diamonds! Look what I have received from the loving King!"

Rosaline asked, "Madame, did anything else come along with that?"

"Nothing but this!" the Princess said, waving a piece of paper. "Yes, as much love in rhyme as would be crammed up in a sheet of paper, written on both sides of the leaf, margin and all, so that he was forced to put his wax seal on the place where he had written the name of Cupid."

"That was the way to make his godhead wax and grow," Rosaline said. "For he has been for five thousand years a boy."

People in this society believed that the world had existed for only 5,000 years, and so Cupid had been in existence all that time, and he had been a boy all that time.

Katherine said, "Yes, and he has been a wily, trouble-making fellow who deserves to be hung on a gallows, too."

"You'll never be friends with him," Rosaline said. "He killed your sister, who died because of Love."

"He made her melancholy, sad, and heavy, and so she died," Katherine said. "Had she been light, like you, of such a merry, nimble, stirring spirit, she might have been a grandmother before she died. And so may you; for a light heart lives long."

The four women were able to make jokes about each other; friends sometimes engage in light teasing and light insults.

Rosaline asked, "What's your dark meaning, mouse, of this light word?"

The word "light" can mean "lighthearted," or it can mean "having light heels." A woman with light heels is a wanton woman.

Katherine replied, "A light condition — disposition — in a dark beauty."

"We need more light to find your meaning out," Rosaline said.

"You'll mar the light by taking it in snuff," Katherine said. "Therefore, I'll darkly end the argument."

When a candle is snuffed, the light is marred — the light goes out. The idiom "to take in snuff" means "to be annoyed."

"Whatever you do, you do it still in the dark," Rosaline said.

One meaning of "do it" is "have sex."

Two meanings of "still" are "always" and "not moving."

"So do not you, for you are a light wench," Katherine said.

Katherine had used "light" to mean "wanton."

Deliberately misinterpreting "light" to refer to her weight, Rosaline replied, "Indeed, I weigh not as much as you, and therefore I am light."

"You weigh me not?" Katherine said, "Oh, that means that you don't care for me."

"I have a great reason for that," Rosaline said, "for 'past cure is still past care.' What cannot be helped is not to be worried about."

The Princess approved of this exchange of witty lines and compared it to a tennis match in which words, not a ball, were volleyed back and forth: "Well bandied both; this is a set of wit well played.

"But Rosaline, you have a favor, too. Who sent it? And what is it?"

By "favor," the Princess meant a "mark of favor or esteem from a lover," aka "love token," but Rosaline deliberately misinterpreted the word as meaning "appearance."

Rosaline said, "I wish you knew. If my face were as fair as yours, my favor would be as great. But be a witness to this" — she held up a piece of paper — "I have love verses, too. I thank Biron for them. The numbers — the poetic meter — are true, and if his numbering — enumeration — of my good points was also true, I would be the fairest goddess walking on the ground. In these lines of love poetry, I am compared to twenty thousand beautiful women. Oh, he has drawn my picture in his letter!"

"Is his picture of you anything like the real you?" the Princess asked.

"There is much likeness in the letters; no likeness at all in the praise," Rosaline replied.

The letters were written with black ink, and Rosaline was black, so the letters and Rosaline were alike. But Rosaline knew, of course, that all the praise heaped on her in the love poem was much more than she deserved. In fact, all of the ladies were amused by the undeserved praise heaped upon them in their love letters.

"You are as beauteous as ink," the Princess said. "That is a good conclusion."

Katherine said, "Rosaline is as fair as a text B in a copy-book."

She was referring a highly ornate gothic capital B in a copybook — such a letter required much black ink.

Rosaline said, "Beware pencils."

The ladies were beginning to metaphorically draw — describe — each other's faces. Such an activity can lead to hurt feelings, even if done humorously.

Rosaline continued, "Let me not die your debtor."

In other words, let me not die without having first repaid you the insult you gave to me and that I owe you.

She continued, "My red dominical, my golden letter, oh, that your face were not so full of O's!"

Katherine's face was pink and her hair was golden — light-colored. A red dominical is a red letter that was used to mark Sundays and feast days in an almanac. Golden letters were also used to mark Sundays and feast days. Katherine had survived smallpox, a disease that left her face bearing O-shaped scars.

The Princess said, "A pox on that jest! And I beshrew all shrews — I scold all scolds!"

She then asked, "But, Katherine, what was sent to you from fair Dumain?"

Katherine replied, "Madam, this glove."

In this society, gloves were ornate and expensive.

The Princess asked, "Didn't he send you two gloves?"

"Yes, madam, and moreover he sent me some thousand verses written by himself, a faithful lover. Those verses are a huge expression of hypocrisy, vilely written, and of profound simplicity — complete foolishness."

Maria said, "This letter and these pearls were sent to me from Longaville. The letter is too long by half a mile."

"I think no less," the Princess said. "Don't you wish in your heart that the pearl necklace was longer and the letter was short?"

Maria wrapped her hands in the necklace and replied, "Yes, or I wish these hands might never part."

The Princess said, "We are wise girls to mock our lovers so."

The four men were wooing the four women in a courtly, old-fashioned way; the women wondered whether they were being mocked. The women preferred a different kind of wooing, one involving real conversation rather than undeserved and extravagant praise in love verses.

Rosaline said, "They are worse fools because they deserve to be mocked by us like this. That same Biron I'll torture before I go back to France. Oh, I wish that I knew he were well and truly captured by love! How I would make him fawn and beg and seek and wait the season — wait until I'm ready — and observe the times — observe the rules — and spend his prodigal wits in bootless, unavailing rhymes and shape his service wholly to my commands and hests and make him proud to make me proud who jests!

"So pair-taunt-like would I oversway and override his state that he should be my fool and I his fate."

"Pair-taunt-like" meant "like holding the winning hand in an old card game called post and pair." A winning hand is a pair-taunt — a double pair royal.

The Princess said, "None are so surely caught, when they are caught, as a wit — an intelligent man — who has turned fool.

"Folly, in wisdom originated, has wisdom's warrant and the help of education and wit's own grace to grace — to do honor to — a learned fool."

In other words, an intelligent man who believes something foolish will use his intelligence and his education to try to show that the foolish thing he believes is actually wise.

Rosaline said, "The blood of youth burns not with such excess as gravity's revolt to wantonness."

In other words, a hot-blooded young man does not burn as fiercely as a serious, mature man who stops being serious and mature so that he can be wanton.

Maria said, "Folly in fools bears not so strong a note as foolery in the wise, when wit does dote, since all the power thereof it does apply to prove, by wit, worth in simplicity."

In other words, a wise man who begins to act like a fool will act more foolishly than a fool because the wise man will use his wisdom to try to prove that it is worthwhile to be simple-minded.

The Princess said, "Here comes Boyet, and mirth is in his face. He is amused by something."

Boyet walked over to the four ladies and said, "Oh, I am stabbed with laughter! I have been laughing so much that my sides hurt. Where's her grace? Where's the Princess?"

The Princess asked, "What is your news, Boyet?"

"Prepare yourself, madam, prepare yourself!" Boyet replied. "Arm yourselves, wenches, arm yourselves! Encounters are being mounted to disturb your peace.

"Lovers, disguised, are approaching you, and they are armed in arguments of love. You'll be surprised and taken off your guard. Muster your wits and stand in your own defense, or hide your heads like cowards and flee from here."

The Princess said, "Saint Denis to Saint Cupid!"

Saint Denis is the patron saint of France.

She continued, "Who are they who charge their breath and voices as if they were charging — loading — weapons against us? Tell us, scout; tell us, spy."

Boyet replied, "Under the cool shade of a sycamore tree, I thought to close my eyes and nap some half an hour, but my purposed rest was interrupted because I saw King Ferdinand and his companions advancing toward that sycamore tree. Warily and carefully I stole into a nearby neighboring thicket, and I overheard what you shall hear over again, and that is, by and by, in disguise they will come here.

"Their herald is Mote, who is a pretty, knavish page, who well by heart has conned his message he will recite to you. Action and accent — the appropriate gestures and correct emphasis of words — they taught him there, telling him, 'Thus you must speak,' and 'thus you must your body bear.'

"And every now and then they expressed a suspicion that being in the presence of your majestic presence would make him forget his part 'for,' said the King, 'an angel you shall see, yet fear not, but speak boldly and audaciously.'

"The boy replied, 'An angel is not evil; I should have feared her had she been a devil.'

"Hearing that, all laughed and clapped him on the shoulder, making the bold wag by their praises bolder.

"One rubbed his elbow like this to express his satisfaction, and he grinned and swore that a better speech was never spoken before.

"Another made the OK sign with his finger and his thumb and then cried, '*Via*! Come on! We will do it, come what will come.'

"The third he capered and danced joyously, and cried, 'All goes well.'

"The fourth turned on the toe and attempted to pirouette, and down he fell.

"With that, they all tumbled on the ground, with a very zealous and profound laughter — but in the midst of this ridiculous amusement the solemn tears of overpowering emotion appeared and checked their folly."

"What?" the Princess asked. "Are they coming to visit us?"

"They are, they are," Boyet replied. "And they will be disguised. They will be dressed like Muscovites or Russians, I believe. Their purpose is to parley and talk, to court, and to dance; and every one will perform a love-feat — a feat done out of love — for his loved one, whom each man will know by the favors — the love tokens — that they formerly did bestow."

"Will they do so?" the Princess asked. "The gallants shall be tasked, for, ladies, we shall each of us be masked and not a man of them shall have the privilege, aka grace, despite their wooing, to see a lady's face. They will see the favors and masks and not our faces, and so they will not know who we really are.

"Rosaline, you shall wear the pendant that King Ferdinand gave to me, and that way the King will court you, thinking that you are his dear. You take the pendant, and give me the love token that Biron gave to you, and that way Biron will take me for Rosaline.

"Katherine and Maria, exchange your favors, too. That way, your lovers will woo the wrong women because they will be deceived by these exchanges of favors."

"Come on, then," Rosaline said. "Wear the favors where they can be easily seen."

Katherine asked, "But in this exchange of favors, what is your intention?"

The Princess said, "The intended result of my intention is to cross their intention. They are doing this only in mocking merriment; they want to make fun of us. And mock for mock is only my intention. They want to make fun of us, but we shall make fun of them.

"They shall unbosom their counsels of love to the wrong loved one, and we will mock them the next occasion that we meet, when, with our faces showing, we shall talk to them and greet them."

Rosaline asked, "But shall we dance, if they ask us to dance?"

"No, we will prefer to die than move a foot," the Princess said. "Nor to their prepared and written-out speech will we give any favor and grace, but while it is spoken each of us will turn away her face."

Feeling sympathy for Mote, Boyet said, "Why, that contempt will kill the speaker's heart, and quite divorce his memory from his part."

"That is why I will do it," the Princess said, "and I have no doubt the rest will never come in, if the speaker be out — if he is at a loss.

"There's no such sport as sport by sport overthrown, to make theirs ours and ours none but our own.

"So shall we stay, mocking intended game, and they, well mocked, will go away with shame."

She wanted to play a practical joke on the men that would trump the practical joke — disguising themselves as Russians — that the men intended to play on her and the other ladies.

A trumpet sounded to announce the arrival of visitors.

Boyet said, "The trumpet sounds. Put on your masks; the men disguised as Russians have come."

The four women put on masks to hide their faces. They also wore love tokens, but not their own.

Some black musicians arrived, along with Mote. Then came King Ferdinand, Biron, Longaville, and Dumain, all of whom were disguised as Russians. They were wearing visors and Russian clothing. A visor is a mask, or a disguise that helps hide one's face.

Mote said, "All hail, the richest beauties on the earth!"

Boyet said, "Beauties no richer than rich taffeta."

The ladies were wearing masks made of taffeta fabric.

Mote continued, "Here is a holy company of the fairest dames —"

The ladies turned their backs to him.

Mote continued, "— who ever turned their ... backs ... to mortal views!"

Biron whispered to Mote, "Not their backs! Their eyes, villain, their eyes!"

Mote said, "— who ever turned their eyes to mortal views! Out —"

Boyet said, "True; Mote is out of countenance indeed. He is disconcerted."

Mote continued, "Out of your favors, Heavenly spirits, vouchsafe not to behold —"

Biron whispered to Mote, "Not 'not to behold'! *Once* to behold, rogue."

Mote continued, "Once to behold with your Sun-beamed eyes ... with your Sun-beamed eyes —"

He was so disconcerted that he was forgetting the speech he had memorized.

Boyet said, "They will not answer to the epithet 'son-beamed.' It would be best to say 'daughter-beamed' eyes."

More complained, "They do not listen to me, and that brings me out of countenance."

Biron said, "Is this your word-perfect recitation of the speech that you promised us? Be gone, you rogue!"

Mote exited.

Rosaline, pretending to be the Princess, said, "What do these strangers want? Find out, Boyet. If they speak our language, we want some plainspoken man to tell us their intentions. Find out what they want."

Boyet asked Biron, "What do you want with the Princess?"

"Nothing but a peaceful and courteous visit," Biron replied.

Rosaline asked, "What do they say they want?"

Boyet replied, "Nothing but a peaceful and courteous visit."

"Why, that they have," Rosaline said, "so tell them to be gone."

Boyet said, "She says, you have what you want, and you may now be gone."

King Ferdinand said, "Say to her, we have measured — traveled — many miles to tread a measure — dance a dance — with her on this grass."

Boyet said to Rosaline, "They say that they have measured many a mile to tread a measure with you on this grass."

"That is not true," Rosaline replied. "Ask them how many inches are in one mile. If they have measured many miles, the measure then of one mile is easily told."

Boyet said, "If to come hither you have measured miles, and many miles, the Princess bids you say how many inches make up one mile."

Biron replied, "Tell her that we measure them by weary steps."

Tired of "translating" the words of the "Russians," Boyet said, "She hears you herself."

Rosaline asked, "How many weary steps, of the many weary miles you have gone over, are numbered in the travel of one mile?"

Biron said, "We number nothing that we spend for you. Our duty is so rich, so infinite, that we may do it always without reckoning numbers. Do us the favor of showing us the sunshine of your face, so that we, like Sun-worshipping savages, may worship it. Take off your mask."

Rosaline said, "My face is only a Moon, and it is clouded, too."

Rosaline's face was a face of night; it was dark. Like the Moon, it shone by reflected light. Rosaline's face reflected the light of her superior, the Princess, whom she was pretending to be. Rosaline's face was clouded; a mask hid it.

King Ferdinand, who thought that Rosaline was the Princess, said, "Blessed are clouds, to do as such clouds do!"

The clouds — the masks — were blessed because they were so close to the Moon — the lady's face, and to ladies' faces in general.

King Ferdinand continued, "Permit, bright Moon, and these your attending stars, to shine, with those clouds removed, upon our watery eyes."

The Moon was known for having an effect on water.

King Ferdinand wanted the ladies to take off their masks.

Rosaline replied, "Oh, vain petitioner! Beg a greater matter; beg for something more important. You now request nothing but Moonshine in the water."

"Moonshine in the water" is an idiom meaning "something foolish."

King Ferdinand said, "Then, in our measure do but permit us one change."

The word "change" was a pun meaning both "one round of dancing" and "one change of the Moon." The change he wanted was that the Moon be unclouded.

He added, "You wanted me to beg for something; this begging is not strange."

"Play, music, then!" Rosaline said. "You must do it soon."

Music began to play, but Rosaline said, "Not yet! No dance! I have changed my mind! Thus change I like the Moon."

"Won't you dance?" King Ferdinand said. "How did you come to be thus estranged and unfriendly?"

"You took the Moon at full, but now she's changed," Rosaline replied.

"Yet still she is the Moon, and I am the man in the Moon," King Ferdinand said.

The King's intentions toward the Princess included marriage and sharing a bed.

Music began to play, and King Ferdinand said, "The music plays; please give some response to it."

He wanted her to dance.

Rosaline said, "Our ears allow us to have a response to music."

"But your legs should do it," King Ferdinand said.

"Since you are strangers and come here by chance, we'll not be nice — we won't stand on formality. Let's hold hands. But we will not dance."

"Why do we hold hands, then?" King Ferdinand asked.

"Only so we can part as friends," Rosaline said.

She then said to the other ladies, "Curtsy, sweet hearts; and so the measure ends."

"More measure of this measure," King Ferdinand said. "Be not nice."

He wanted the music to continue, and he wanted to dance, and he felt that the "Princess" — the masked Rosaline — was being nice, aka shy or coy. He also wanted to dance because some dances included kissing.

"We can afford to do no more at such a price," Rosaline said.

She was unwilling to dance with and to kiss King Ferdinand.

"Prize you yourselves," King Ferdinand requested. "Put your own price on yourselves. What buys your company?"

"Only your absence buys our company," Rosaline said.

"That can never be," King Ferdinand said. "If we Moscovites are absent and away from you, we cannot enjoy your company, and so we cannot buy your company."

"Then we cannot be bought," Rosaline said, "and so, adieu. I say adieu twice to your visor, and half of once to you."

A visor is a mask, or a disguise that helps hide one's face. Rosaline was strongly hinting that she knew that King Ferdinand was in disguise. By saying adieu twice to the King's visor, she was saying that she would like for him to get rid of the disguise. By saying adieu only half of once to him, she was saying that she was rejecting him, but it was not a major rejection. Under different circumstances, such as meeting face to face with no masks and no disguises worn and no games played, the ladies and the gentlemen could possibly get along very well together.

"If you decline to dance, then let's talk some more," King Ferdinand requested.

"In private, then," Rosaline replied.

"I am best pleased with that," King Ferdinand said, and the two withdrew to a private spot and talked quietly.

Biron, disguised as a Russian, said to the masked Princess, whom he thought was his beloved, Rosaline, "White-handed mistress, I request one sweet word with you."

The Princess replied, "Honey, and milk, and sugar; there are three sweet words."

"No, then, let's make it two treys, as if we were throwing dice, and if you grow so nice and precise, I'll make my three sweet words metheglin, wort, and malmsey. These are three strong sweet drinks. Well run, dice! There's half-a-dozen sweets."

"Here is a seventh sweet word: adieu," the Princess said. "Since you play games while playing a game, I'll play no more with you. You cog the dice."

To "cog the dice" is to "load the dice," and so it means to defraud, deceive, and tell lies.

"One word in secret," Biron said.

"Let it not be sweet," the Princess said.

"You grieve my gall," Biron said. "You hit me in a sore spot."

"Gall!" the Princess said. "Bitter."

"And therefore suitable," Biron said.

Gall is bitter, so "bitter" is a suitable word for "gall." Biron was much disappointed in his reception by "Rosaline," and so he was bitter.

Biron and the Princess withdrew to a private spot and talked quietly.

Dumain said to Maria, who was wearing the love token that Dumain had given to Katherine, "Will you permit me to exchange a word with you?"

"Name it," Maria said.

"Fair lady —" Dumain began.

"Do you say so? Is that your word that you wish to exchange?" Maria said. "Fair *lord* — take that in exchange for your fair *lady*."

"If it will please you, let us talk as much in private, and then I'll bid you adieu."

Dumain and Maria withdrew to a private spot and talked quietly.

Katherine said to Longaville, who thought that she was Maria, "Was your mask made without a tongue?"

Some masks were held in place by a "tongue" — a piece protruding into the mouth and held by the teeth.

Katherine was asking Longaville why he was so quiet.

Longaville replied, "I know the reason, lady, why you ask."

"Oh, I long to know what you think is the reason! Quickly, sir; I long."

"You have a double tongue within your mask, and you would give my speechless mask half," Longaville replied.

A double tongue is a deceptive tongue.

Katherine said, "'Veal,' quoth the Dutchman. Is not 'veal' a calf?"

"Veal" is the English word "well" pronounced with a Dutch accent.

Katherine's last word before "veal" had been "long": "long veal." She was playing with the name "Longaville."

A calf is a fool. She was calling Longaville a fool and so was teasing him.

"A calf, fair lady!" Longaville said.

"No, a fair lord calf," Katherine replied.

"Let's part the word."

Parting the word "calf" gave "ca" and "lf." Katherine's name began with the hard-c "ca" sound, and the word "half" ended with "lf."

Also, if they were to part the word, then half of the word would apply to both of them; half would be Katherine's, and half would be Longaville's. Longaville was saying, in other words, if I am a calf, aka fool, then so are you.

"No, I'll not be your half," Katherine replied.

She was saying that she did not want to be his better half, aka wife.

She added, "Take all, and wean it; it may prove to be an ox."

An ox is a castrated bull.

Longaville said, "Look how you butt yourself in these sharp mocks. Will you give horns, chaste lady? Do not do that."

If Katherine were to give horns after she was married, she would be giving her husband horns — that is, she would make him a cuckold. If she were to do that, she would be butting herself — acting in such a way that would get her a bad reputation. And by being insulting to Longaville right now, she risked getting a reputation as a shrew.

Katherine said, "Then die while you are still a calf, before your horns grow."

"Give me one word in private with you, before I die," Longaville said.

"Bleat softly then," Katherine said. "The butcher hears you cry."

Longaville and Katherine withdrew to a private spot and talked quietly.

Boyet, who had heard Katherine teasing Longaville and who had heard all the "Russian" men being verbally mocked by the ladies, said, "The tongues of mocking wenches are as sharp and keen as is the razor's invisible edge, cutting a smaller hair than may be seen, above the sense of sense — beyond the ability of the senses to perceive — so sensible seems their conversation. Their witticisms have wings fleeter than arrows, bullets, wind, thought, and swifter things."

"Not one word more, my maids," Rosaline said. "Break off all conversation, break it off."

"By Heaven, we are all dry-beaten with pure scoff and mockery!" Biron said.

To be "dry-beaten" was to be thoroughly beaten but without the shedding of blood. This had been a verbal battle that the ladies had decisively won; it had not been a physical battle.

"Farewell, mad wenches," a greatly disappointed King Ferdinand said. "You have simple — foolish and unsophisticated — wits."

"Twenty adieus, my Muscovites of the frozen north," the Princess said.

King Ferdinand, the lords, and the black musicians departed.

The Princess said, "Are these the breeds of wits that are so admired?"

Boyet said, "They are candles, and your sweet breaths have blown them out."

"Well-liking wits they have," Rosaline said. "They are gross, gross; they are fat, fat."

In other words, she was saying that the "visiting Russians" — the lords — are fatheads. "Well-liking" meant "liking well" — metaphorically, the brains of the "visiting Russians" liked well their food, which made them fat and dulled their wit.

"Oh, poverty in wit, Kingly-poor flout!" the Princess said, thinking of King Ferdinand's insult that the ladies had simple — foolish and unsophisticated — wits. His jeer was unworthy of a King; if Kings must insult, they should be wittier than King Ferdinand had shown himself to be.

The Princess asked, "Do you think that they will hang themselves tonight? Or ever, except while wearing masks, show their faces? This pert, cheeky Biron was quite out of countenance. He was quite disconcerted."

"Oh, they were all in lamentable cases!" Rosaline said.

"Cases" meant both "conditions" and "masks."

She added, "The King was ready to weep because he so much wanted a good word, which he did not get."

The Princess said, "Biron did swear himself out of all suit. He began to swear and ceased to woo."

"Dumain was at my service," Maria said, "and his sword was, too. '*Non point*,' said I, and my servant immediately was mute."

"*Non point*" was French for "No point," which has two meanings.

Katherine said, "Lord Longaville said that I overcame his heart; and do you know what he called me?"

"Qualm, perhaps," the Princess said.

Longaville may have felt that she had conquered his heart, but after being insulted by her, he probably felt a qualm — a sudden attack of sickness — that came over him and affected his heart.

"Yes, indeed," Katherine said.

"Go, sickness that you are!" the Princess said. "Ha!"

She was joking that since Katherine was "ill," she should leave.

The ladies were not amused by the wit of the men.

Rosaline said, "Well, better wits — more intelligent and wittier men — have worn plain statute-caps."

By statute, people of low status, such as apprentices, had to wear simple woolen caps on certain days.

Rosaline said, "But will you listen to this? The King is my sworn love."

"And quick and lively Biron has pledged his faith to me," the Princess said.

"And Longaville was born to be my servant," Katherine said.

"Dumain is mine, as surely as bark is on trees," Maria said.

"Madam, and pretty mistresses, listen to me," Boyet said. "Quickly they will again be here as their own selves, with no disguises, for it can never be that they will swallow and digest this harsh indignity. They cannot endure such rejection and will return here to try to improve their reception by you."

"Will they return here?" the Princess asked.

"They will, they will, God knows," Boyet said, "and they will leap for joy, although they are lame with blows. Therefore exchange the favors; and, when they return, blow like sweet roses in this summer air."

"By "blow," Boyet meant "burst into blossom."

The Princess, not understanding, asked, "How blow? How blow? What does that mean? Speak in such a way that I can understand you."

Boyet said, "Fair ladies masked are roses in their bud. Dismasked, their damask — deep pink — sweet commixture of red and white shown, are angels moving aside clouds and becoming visible, or roses blown in full flower."

"Avaunt, perplexity!" the Princess said. "Away, riddling words!"

She preferred a more easily understood way of speaking.

She asked, "What shall we do, if they return as themselves to woo us?"

Rosaline replied, "Good madam, if by me you'll be advised, let's continue to mock them; we can do that as well when they are not disguised as when they are disguised. Let us complain to them what fools were here, disguised like Muscovites, in unshapely clothing, and wonder who they were and to what end their shallow spectacles and their vilely penned, badly written prologue, and their rough and ridiculous way of bearing themselves was presented at our tent to us."

Seeing the lords, now undisguised, returning, Boyet said, "Ladies, withdraw. The gallants are at hand."

"Dash to our tents, as quickly as deer run over land," the Princess said.

The ladies — the Princess, Rosaline, Maria, and Katherine — ran to their tents.

King Ferdinand, Biron, Longaville, and Dumain, now wearing their usual clothing and no disguises, walked over to Boyet.

King Ferdinand asked him, "Fair sir, God save you! Where's the Princess?"

"Gone to her tent," Boyet replied, "Will it please your majesty to command me to do any service to her thither? Do you want me to take a message to her?"

"Say that I would like for her to permit me to speak to her one word," King Ferdinand said.

"I will," Boyet said, "and she will listen to you, I know, my lord."

Boyet left to perform his errand.

In a bad mood, Biron criticized Boyet:

"This fellow pecks up wit as pigeons peck up peas, and utters it again when God does please. He is wit's peddler, and he retails his wares at wakes and drunken wassails, meetings, markets, and fairs; and we who sell wit by the gross, the Lord knows, don't have the grace to grace it with such a show as Boyet.

"This gallant pins the wenches on his sleeve. If he had been Adam, he would have tempted Eve, instead of Eve tempting Adam in the Garden of Eden.

"He can carve meat at the table, too, and lisp and speak in an affected manner. Why, this is he who kissed his hand away in courtesy."

In some social situations in this society, a gentleman would kiss his own hand.

Biron continued, "This man is the ape of form, the imitator of those with good etiquette, he is Monsieur the Nice, and so it is the case that when he plays at backgammon, he chides the dice using honorable — not swear — words.

"He can sing a middle-range — neither high nor low — part in a song quite respectfully, and when it comes to performing the duties of a gentleman usher, no one can beat him.

"The ladies call him sweet, and the stairs, as he treads on them, kiss his feet.

"This is the flower that smiles on everyone in order to show that his teeth are as white as a walrus' tusk.

"And consciences, that will not die in debt, pay him the due of calling him 'honey-tongued Boyet.'"

King Ferdinand said, "I say with my heart that I wish there were a blister on his sweet tongue, because he is the man who disconcerted Mote, Armado's page, so much that he could not say his part!"

Seeing Boyet returning, Biron said, "See where it comes! Courteous behavior, what were you until this madman showed you? And what are you now?"

Boyet ushered the Princess, Rosaline, Maria, and Katherine into the presence of the lords.

King Ferdinand said to the Princess, "All hail, sweet madam, and fair time of day!"

By "hail," King Ferdinand meant "greetings," but the Princess deliberately misinterpreted "hail" to refer to the principal ingredient in a hailstorm, which is foul weather, not fair weather.

She said, "'Fair' in 'all hail' is foul, I believe. Don't call a hailstorm fair."

King Ferdinand, who knew that she was deliberately misinterpreting his words, said, "Construe my speeches better, if you may."

"Then give me better wishes," the Princess said. "I give you permission to do that."

"We came to visit you," King Ferdinand said, "and we intend now to lead you to our court; please give us permission to do so."

"This field shall hold me; and so you will hold and keep your vow. Neither God, nor I, delights in perjured men."

"Don't rebuke me for that which you yourself provoke," King Ferdinand said. "The virtue of your eye makes me break my oath."

By "virtue," King Ferdinand meant "power," but again the Princess deliberately misinterpreted him.

She replied, "You misname the word 'virtue'; 'vice' is the word you should have spoken, for virtue's operation never breaks men's good faith.

"Now by my maiden honor, yet as pure as the unsullied lily, I protest that even though I would endure a world of torments, I would not yield to be a guest in your house, so much I hate to be a cause of breaking any Heavenly oaths that have been vowed with integrity."

King Ferdinand said, "Oh, you have lived in desolation here, unseen, unvisited, much to our shame."

"Not so, my lord," the Princess replied, "It is not so, I swear. We have had pastimes here and pleasant entertainment. A mess — a group of four — of Russians left us only recently."

"What, madam! Russians!" King Ferdinand said, pretending to be surprised.

"Yes, indeed, my lord. They were trim gallants, full of courtship — courtliness and courting — and of stateliness."

"Madam, tell the truth," Rosaline said, preparing to criticize the Russians and therefore the lords. "What she said is not so, my lord. My lady, in accordance with the good manners of these days, out of courtesy gives the Russians undeserved praise.

"We four ladies were indeed confronted with four men wearing Russian clothing. Here they stayed an hour, and talked apace — quickly — and during that hour, my lord, they did not bless us with one happy, well-chosen, felicitous word.

"I dare not call them fools; but this I think, when fools are thirsty, fools would like to have a drink. I don't think these Russians know enough to do that."

"This jest is dry to me," Biron said to Rosaline.

Of course, he did not think that the Russians were fools.

Biron continued, "Fair gentle sweet, your wit makes wise things foolish. When we greet, with eyes best seeing, Heaven's fiery eye, by light we lose light — the Sun blinds us. Your capacity — your intellect — is of that nature that compared to your huge store of intelligence, wise things seem foolish and rich things seem to be poor."

Rosaline replied, "This proves you to be wise and rich, for in my eye —"

Biron finished the joke for her: "— I am a fool, and full of poverty. And if you think that of me, then according to what I said, I am wise and I am full of wealth."

Rosaline said, "Make sure that you take only what belongs to you; it is a fault to snatch words from my tongue."

Biron publicly confessed his love for her: "Oh, I am yours, and all that I possess!"

"All the fool is mine?" Rosaline asked.

"I cannot give you less," Biron said.

"Which of the visors was it that you wore?" she asked him.

Disconcerted, Biron said, "Where? When? What visor? Why do you ask me this?"

Rosaline replied, "Where? There. When? Then. What visor? That superfluous, unnecessary visor that hid the worse and showed the better face."

Realizing immediately that ladies knew that they, the lords, had been disguised as the visiting Russians, King Ferdinand said, "We have been detected; they'll mock us now without pity."

Dumain said, "Let us confess and say it was a jest."

"Dumbfounded, my lord?" the Princess asked King Ferdinand. "Why does your highness look sad?"

Rosaline cried, "Help, hold his brows! He'll faint!"

She said to Biron, "Why do you look so pale? You are sea-sick, I think, having come from Moscow."

Biron said to Rosaline, "Thus the stars pour down plagues for perjury. We are being punished for violating our oath. Can any face of brass brazen it out any longer?

"Here stand I, lady, dart your skill at me — shoot your verbal weapons at me. Bruise me with scorn, confound me with a jeer, thrust your sharp wit quite through my ignorance, cut me to pieces with your keen, sharp intellect, and I will never more ask you to dance, nor will I ever again in Russian clothing try to be your servant.

"Oh, I will never trust to prewritten speeches, nor to the motion of a schoolboy's — Mote's — tongue, nor ever come in a disguise to my loved one, nor woo in rhyme, like a blind harper's song!"

People with handicaps such as blindness sometimes played musical instruments to make a living.

Biron continued to reject ways of wooing that were affected:

"Fancy taffeta phrases, silken terms precise, three-layered hyperboles, spruce affectation, pedantic figures of speech — these summer-flies have filled me full of maggoty ostentation. I forswear them."

Biron now vowed to woo in a different way, one more honest and less affected:

"I here protest, by this, Rosaline's white glove — how white the hand is, God knows! — that henceforth my wooing mind shall be expressed in russet yeas and honest kersey noes. I will speak simply and understandably: I will say yes, and I will say no. My language will be plainspoken, like the plain russet and kersey clothing worn by people who don't wear fancy clothing.

"And, to begin, wench — so God help me, la! — my love for you is sound, *sans* crack or flaw."

Biron had begun to immediately implement his new way of wooing. He would not call her hand — which was black — white. He would use no love-poetry terms, not now, although his speech would still profess love for Rosaline. She was no longer a goddess; he affectionately called her a wench.

And he used the homespun interjection "la," rather than a fancy word. But he did make one mistake, which Rosaline immediately identified: He used the French word "*sans*," which means "without."

She said, "Talk to me sans '*sans*,' please."

He replied, "I still have a touch of the old madness. Bear with me, I am sick; I'll leave my old madness behind by degrees.

"Wait, let us see. Write, 'Lord have mercy on us,' on those three — King Ferdinand, Longaville, and Dumain — they are infected with the same madness; in their hearts it lies; they have the plague, and they caught it from the eyes of you ladies. These lords have been visited with sickness; you are not free, for the Lord's tokens on you I do see."

The sentence "Lord have mercy on us" was written on the doors of houses in which were people infected with the plague.

Many people in this society believed that the plague was a visitation of the wrath of God.

The lords were all infected with love madness, and Biron joked that ladies were not free of that plague. "The Lord's tokens" were physical signs of being infected with the plague, and of course, "the lords' tokens" were the love-tokens the lords had given the ladies and that the ladies were now wearing.

The Princess replied, "No, they are free who gave these tokens to us."

By "free," she meant "generous."

Biron said, "Our states are forfeit: Seek not to undo us."

One meaning of his sentence was this: "Our estates are forfeited and subject to confiscation: Seek not to ruin us."

Another meaning of his sentence was this: "We have forfeited much of our honor through our silly actions: Seek not to disconcert us more by continuing to mock us."

Rosaline said, "It can't be true that you are forfeit, for how can it be true that you are forfeit, since you are those who sue?"

The lords were suing — begging — the ladies for their love. They were suitors pleading for love.

Biron said, "Peace! Quiet! For I will not have to do with you."

This meant both "I won't have anything to do with you" and "I won't have sex with you." Biron was discouraged.

"Nor shall you not if I do as I intend," Rosaline replied. She was unwilling to have sex with him at this time. But the double negative hinted that perhaps at some time she would be willing.

Biron said to the other lords, "Speak for yourselves; my wit is at an end. I have nothing more to say."

King Ferdinand asked the Princess, "Teach us, sweet madam, for our rude transgression some fair excuse. Tell us how we can excuse and make up for what we have done."

"The fairest way is confession," she replied.

Giving him an opportunity to confess, she asked, "Weren't you here — disguised — just a short while ago?"

"Madam, I was," King Ferdinand admitted.

"And were you in your right mind?"

"I was, fair madam."

"When you then were here, what did you whisper in your lady's ear?" the Princess asked.

"That more than all the world I did respect and value her."

"When she shall challenge this and say that you did not say that to her, you will reject her," the Princess said.

"Upon my honor, no," King Ferdinand replied. "I swear upon my honor."

"Peace! Be quiet! Don't! Having already broken your oath once, you won't hesitate to break it again."

The first oath King Ferdinand had broken was to stay from women for three years.

"Despise me, when I break this oath of mine," King Ferdinand said.

"I will," the Princess said to the King, "and therefore keep your oath."

The Princess then asked, "Rosaline, what did the Russian whisper in your ear?"

She replied, "Madam, he swore that he did regard me as dear as precious eyesight, and he did value me more than all this world, and he added to all this that he would wed me, or else he would die my lover."

"May God give you joy of him!" the Princess said. "I hope that you two will be happy together! The noble King Ferdinand will very honorably uphold his word — he will do what he swore to do."

King Ferdinand objected, "What do you mean, madam? By my life, by my truth and honor, I swear that I never swore to this lady such an oath. I never said that I loved her and would marry her."

"By Heaven, I swear you did," Rosaline said, "and to plainly confirm it, look at this."

She held up a small love token — not the pendant the King had previously given to the Princess — and said, "You gave me this, but take it, sir, back again."

King Ferdinand said, "I gave both my faithful love and this love token to the Princess. I knew who she was by the jewel she was wearing on her sleeve."

The jewel was the pendant depicting a lady with a border made of diamonds. One meaning of "jewel" is "precious thing."

"Pardon me, sir," the Princess said. "Rosaline was wearing this jewel. And Lord Biron, I thank him, is my dear lover."

She asked Biron, "Will you have me, or your pearl, again?"

Biron's love token to Rosaline was a pearl. One meaning of "pearl" is "precious thing."

Biron replied, "I want nothing to do with either. I give up both of them.

"I see the trick that was played on us. Here there was an agreement, a plot. You knew ahead of time about the merriment we had planned — to dress up like Russians — and you plotted to spoil it like you would a Christmas comedy — many people jeer at actors.

"Some carry-tale, some gossip, some please-man, some yes-man, some slight zany, some lightweight comic servant, some mumble-news, some trencher-knight, some person who conquers large meals, some common Dick, some person who smiles his cheeks into wrinkles and knows that the trick is to make my lady laugh when she's disposed to laugh, told you ladies beforehand what we intended to do.

"Once that was disclosed, you ladies exchanged favors and put on masks, and then we lords, following the signs of the love tokens, wooed just the sign — not the substance — of whichever woman we loved. We pledged our love not to the woman we loved, but to the woman whom we thought was the woman we loved.

"Now, to add more terror to our original perjury, we are again forsworn, in will and error.

"That is pretty much what happened."

Biron knew who was the tattletale. He had already criticized Boyet as an affected dandy who kept ladies entertained.

He said to Boyet, "And aren't you the one who ruined our sport and made us thus untrue to our vows?

"Don't you know my lady's foot by the squire — uh, square? Don't you have her measure? Don't you know how to please her?"

A square is a measuring instrument. "My lady" was a generic term for an upper-class woman. As a ladies' man, Boyet had my lady's measure, and he knew how to please her and how to squire — escort — her. The Princess, and especially Rosaline, could easily have thought that "my lady" referred to her, but they ignored that interpretation.

The word "foot" was similar to the French word "*foutre*," which means "fuck."

Biron continued, "Don't you laugh upon the apple — the pupil — of her eye? Don't you keep her entertained so that you can be at the center of her attention? Don't you laugh with her at the things she likes to laugh at?"

One meaning of the word "eye" was "vagina." Biron was saying that Boyet laughed as he had vaginal sex.

Biron had used the words "squire" and "apple." In this society, "an apple-squire" meant "a pimp."

Biron continued, "Don't you stand between her back, sir, and the fire, holding a trencher, and jesting merrily?"

One meaning of what Biron had said was that Boyet acted as a fire screen and kept my lady from getting too hot as she faced away from him.

Another meaning involved "stand" as "erection" and "fire" as "vagina." With that meaning, Boyet stood behind my lady and put his "stand" in the hole between the woman's "fire" and her back. Often, the word "trencher" means "plate," but it can also mean "knife." Here, the trencher was a phallic symbol. One meaning of "to jest" is "to amuse oneself and others."

Biron continued, "You put our page — Mote — out of countenance.

"Go on and mock me, you are allowed. You are a fool, and licensed fools are allowed to say whatever they want.

"Die whenever you will, a smock — a petticoat — shall be your shroud. You shall be buried like the woman you are."

In this society, the word "die" also meant "have an orgasm." Biron was also saying that Boyet had sex while wearing women's clothing.

Boyet smiled derisively at Biron, who said, "You leer upon me, do you? There's an eye that wounds like a leaden sword."

A leaden sword was not a real sword; it was a property sword — one used in theatrical productions. (Wooden swords were also used as stage props.) It was also another phallic symbol. *Vagina* is Latin for "sheath" — a good place to put a sword.

Boyet replied, "Very merrily has this brave manage, this career, this gallop of words at full speed, been run."

Biron said, "Lo, he is tilting straight! Peace! I have done. Quiet! I have finished!"

One meaning of "tilting straight" is "immediately going back to his encounters (of wit)."

Another meaning of "tilting straight" is "immediately going back to thrusting (with his penis)."

Costard walked over to the group.

Biron said to Costard, "Welcome, pure wit! You have stopped a fair fray — a good fight."

Costard said, "Oh, Lord, sir, they want to know whether the three Worthies shall come in or not."

"Are there only three?"

"No, sir; but it is vara fine, for every one pursents three."

"Vara" was a dialect word meaning "very," and "pursents" meant a combination of "presents" and "represents."

Costard was saying that each of the three people would appear as three different Worthies.

People who know arithmetic would deduce there would be nine — the normal number — Worthies in all.

Biron said, "And three times thrice is nine."

Costard objected, "Not so, sir; let me correct you, sir; I hope it is not so.

"You cannot beg us, sir. I can assure you, sir, that we know what we know."

By "you cannot beg us," Costard meant that he was not a fool. Sometimes an incompetent person would inherit money and property, and that person's relatives would beg the law court to be appointed guardians of the fool so they could manage that fool's money and possessions. "To beg a fool" meant "to petition the Court of Wards to get custody of an incompetent person." "To beg someone for a fool" meant "to take that person for a fool."

One way of testing a person's competence was to ask that person to do simple arithmetic.

Costard continued, "I hope, sir, three times thrice, sir —"

Biron interrupted, "— is not nine?"

Costard replied, "Let me correct you, sir. We know to how much it does amount."

Biron said, "By Jove, I always took three threes for nine."

"Oh, Lord, sir, it would be a pity if you would have to get your living by reckoning, sir," Costard said.

"How much is it?" Biron asked.

"Oh, Lord, sir, the parties themselves, the actors, sir, will show to how much it does amount. As for my own part, I am, as they say, but to parfect one man in one poor man, Pompion the Great, sir."

"Parfect" was a combination of "present" and "perfect." Costard was supposed to be word-perfect as he presented Pompion the Great.

Costard had said that each of three men would present three Worthies. Perhaps only one of the Worthies Costard was to present was a speaking part. But actually he was wrong about the number of people presenting the Worthies: Five people presented the first five Worthies.

By "Pompion the Great," Costard meant Pompey the Great, a military and political leader of the late Roman Republic. Pompey first cooperated with and then opposed Julius Caesar, who triumphed over him.

In this society, a "pompion" was a pumpkin.

Biron asked, "Are you one of the Worthies?"

Costard replied, "It pleased them to think me worthy of Pompion the Great. As for my own part, I know not the rank of the Worthy, but I am to stand for and represent him."

Biron said, "Go, tell them to get ready to present the Worthies."

"We will turn it finely off, sir," Costard said. "We will take some care. We will skillfully perform the Worthies."

King Ferdinand said, "Biron, they will shame us with a bad performance. Let them not perform the Nine Worthies."

"We are shame-proof, my lord," Biron said. "We cannot be shamed any more than we already have, and it is a wise move to have now performed a worse show than the one already performed by the King and his company."

"I say they shall not come here and present the Nine Worthies," King Ferdinand said.

"No, my good lord, let me overrule you now," the Princess said. "That sport best pleases that does least know how to please — where zeal strives to content and please, and the content of the play dies in the zeal of those who present it."

Performers can be so determined to make the audience approve of their performance that their overacting ruins their performance. Nevertheless, the audience can be amused by the overacting.

The Princess continued, "Their form confounded makes most form in mirth, when great things laboring perish in their birth."

She meant that much humor can be found when a great enterprise goes badly wrong.

Biron said to King Ferdinand, "That is a good description of our sport, my lord. The ladies found much humor in our pretending to be Russians."

Don Adriana de Armado walked over to the group and said to King Ferdinand, who at his coronation had been anointed with holy oil, "Anointed, I implore so much expense of your royal sweet breath as will utter a brace of words."

A brace of words is a pair of words. In other words, Armado wanted a short private conversation with the King. The two men went aside and talked together. Costard gave King Ferdinand a paper.

The Princess asked Biron, "Does this man serve God?"

"Why do you ask?"

"He does not speak like a man whom God made," the Princess replied.

Indeed, Armado did not speak like an ordinary human being.

Armado said to King Ferdinand, "That is all one, my fair, sweet, honey monarch; for, I protest, the schoolmaster is exceedingly fantastical; he is too, too vain, too, too vain, but we will put it, as they say, to *fortuna de la guerra*. I wish you the peace of mind, most royal couplement!"

The King had expressed some worries about the presentation of the Nine Worthies, but Armado tried to reassure him and also said that they should leave it up to the *fortuna de la guerra* — the fortunes of war. The most royal couplement was the most royal couple: the King and the Princess.

Armado exited.

King Ferdinand said, "Here is likely to be a good company of Worthies. Armado will represent Hector of Troy. The country swain Costard will represent Pompey the Great. The parish curate Sir Nathaniel will represent Alexander the Great. Armado's page, Mote, will represent Hercules. The pedant, Holofernes, will represent Judas Maccabaeus.

"And if these four Worthies in their first show thrive, these four will change habits, and present the other five."

Biron objected, "There are five Worthies in the first show."

"You are deceived," King Ferdinand said. "That is not so."

He had miscounted, or he was saying that these five people were unworthy and incapable of presenting five Worthies.

Biron pointed out, "The pedant Holofernes, the braggart Armado, the hedge-priest Sir Nathaniel, the fool Costard, and the boy Mote — apart from a throw in the dice game *novum*, the whole world cannot again pick out five such, take each one in his vein, aka take each one for what he is."

A hedge-priest is an uneducated priest.

In the game of *novum*, throws of five and nine are significant.

Seeing Costard approaching, King Ferdinand said, "The ship is under sail, and here she comes amain — at full speed."

Costard, dressed as Pompey the Great, said, "I am Pompey —"

Unfortunately, he tripped and fell on the ground.

Boyet punned, "You lie, you are not he."

Costard said again, "I am Pompey —"

Boyet said, "With a leopard's head on your knee."

In this society, people honored ancient heroes by ascribing to them coats of arms. Pompey's "coat of arms" included a leopard's head. Costard was carrying a prop shield on which was a leopard's head; Costard was resting the shield on his knee.

Biron complimented Boyet, "Well said, old mocker. I must become friends with you."

Costard said, "I am Pompey, Pompey surnamed the Big —"

Dumain corrected him: "The Great."

Costard said, "You are correct. It is 'Great,' sir. I am Pompey surnamed the Great, who often on the battlefield, with targe and shield, did make my foe to sweat."

A targe is a light shield.

Costard continued, "And travelling along this coast, I here am come by chance, and lay my arms before the legs of this sweet lass of France.

"If your ladyship would say, 'Thanks, Pompey,' I have finished my part."

The Princess of France said, "Great thanks, great Pompey."

Costard said, "My performance was not worth so much, but I hope I was word-perfect. I did make a little mistake in 'Great.'"

Biron said, "I bet my hat against a halfpenny that Pompey proves to be the best Worthy."

This was not much of a compliment. Biron was saying the other performances of Worthies would be worse than Costard's performance of Pompey.

Sir Nathaniel, costumed as Alexander the Great, stepped forward and said, "When in the world I lived, I was the world's commander. By east, west, north, and south, I spread my conquering might. My scutcheon plainly declares that I am Alisander —"

A scutcheon is an escutcheon — a painted shield.

Boyet interrupted, "Your nose says no, you are not Alexander the Great, because your nose stands too straight."

Alexander the Great, conqueror of the known world, had a habit of holding his head at an angle. He also was reputed to have had an aquiline nose — one that is hooked or curved. Boyet could also have had in mind the story that Caesar Augustus once visited the preserved corpse of Alexander. Bending down to kiss Alexander's forehead, Caesar Augustus accidentally broke Alexander's nose.

Biron said to Boyet, "Your nose smells 'no' in this, most tender-smelling knight."

Alexander the Great's body and breath were said to smell sweet; Biron was saying that Boyet's nose could tell that Sir Nathaniel's body and breath did not smell sweet.

The Princess said, "The conqueror is dismayed. Proceed, good Alexander."

Sir Nathaniel said, "When in the world I lived, I was the world's commander —"

Boyet said, "Most true, that is right; you were so, Alisander."

Biron said to Costard, "Pompey the Great —"

Costard replied, "I am your servant, as is Costard."

Biron said, "Take away the conqueror; take away Alisander."

Costard said to Sir Nathaniel, "Oh, sir, you have overthrown Alisander the conqueror! You will be scraped out of the painted cloth for this."

Painted cloths were decorative wall hangings, many of which depicted the Nine Worthies. Because of Sir Nathaniel's poor performance, Alexander the Great was in danger of having his image removed from these painted wall hangings.

Costard continued, "Your lion, that holds his pole-axe sitting on a close-stool, will be given to Ajax the Great: he will be the ninth Worthy."

The coat of arms ascribed to Alexander the Great depicted a lion seated on a throne and holding a battle-ax. Costard got part of this wrong: He said the lion was seated on a close-stool — a toilet.

Ajax the Great was a Greek warrior who was second only to Achilles in the Trojan War. Ajax' name, unfortunately, was pronounced much like "a jakes" — "jakes" is an archaic word for "toilet."

Sir Nathaniel was unable to speak, probably because he was disconcerted.

Costard said, "A conqueror, and afraid to speak! Run away for shame, Alisander!"

Sir Nathaniel stepped to the side.

Costard said, "There, if it shall please you, is a foolish mild man. He is an honest man, you see, and soon dashed."

"Dashed" meant "abashed."

Costard continued, "He is a marvelous good neighbor, indeed, and a very good bowler in the game of bowls, but as for the part of Alisander — alas, you see how it is — he is a little overparted. He does not quite measure up to the part. But there are Worthies a-coming who will speak their mind in some other sort."

Holofernes stepped forward, costumed as Judas Maccabaeus, the Hebrew warrior. Mote also stepped forward, costumed as the young Hercules.

Holofernes said, "Great Hercules is presented by this imp, whose club killed Cerberus, that three-headed *canus*, and when he was a babe, a child, a shrimp, thus did he strangle serpents in his *manus*."

"*Manus*" is Latin for "hands"; "*canis*," not "*canus*," is Latin for "dog." Either Holofernes wanted the word to rhyme with "*manus*," or he had made a mistake in his Latin.

Holofernes continued, "*Quoniam* he seems to be in minority, *ergo* I come with this apology."

"*Quoniam*" is Latin for "since"; "*ergo*" is Latin for "therefore." By "in minority," Holofernes meant "a child, a minor." An apology is an explanation; Holofernes was explaining why a minor was presenting Hercules.

Holofernes said to Mote, "Keep some state — stateliness — in thy exit, and vanish."

Mote stepped to the side.

Holofernes said, "I am Judas —"

Dumain said, "A Judas!"

Holofernes said, "Not Judas Iscariot, sir, not the betrayer of Jesus Christ. Judas I am, yclept Maccabaeus."

"Yclept" is an archaic word meaning "called."

Dumain said, "Judas Maccabaeus clipped is plain Judas."

"Clipped" can mean "abbreviated" or "embraced."

Biron said, "A kissing traitor."

Judas Iscariot had betrayed Jesus by embracing and kissing him. This identified Jesus to the people who arrested him.

Biron then asked Holofernes, "How can you prove that you are Judas?"

Holofernes said, "I am Judas —"

"The more shame for you, Judas," Dumain said.

"What do you intend by saying that, sir?" Holofernes said.

Boyet said, "To make Judas hang himself."

Holofernes said, "You go first, sir. You are my elder."

Biron said, "That's a good comeback. Judas was hanged on an elder tree."

With dignity, Holofernes said, "I will not be put out of countenance."

Biron replied, "Because you have no face."

Holofernes pointed to his face and asked, "What is this?"

Unfortunately for him, this provided an opportunity for some male audience members to insult him.

Boyet said, "It is a cittern-head."

A cittern was a musical instrument that resembled a guitar. Its head was often carved into a grotesque face and head.

Dumain said, "It is the head of a bodkin."

A bodkin was a ladies' hairpin; the head of the hairpin was often decorated.

Biron said, "It is a Death's face — a skull — in a ring."

Longaville said, "It is the face on an old Roman coin, scarcely able to be seen because it is so worn."

Boyet said, "It is the pommel of Caesar's falchion. It is the carved hilt of Caesar's sword."

Dumain said, "It is the carved-bone face on a gunpowder flask made of bone."

Biron said, "It is Saint George's half-cheek portrait — his profile — carved on a brooch."

Dumain said, "Yes, a brooch made of lead."

Such a brooch was inexpensive compared to other brooches. Tradesmen advertised their trade with a brooch worn in their hat.

Biron said, "Yes, and worn in the cap of a tooth-drawer."

A tooth-drawer was a primitive dentist. Such a job was low-status, and so the dentist advertised who he was with a less-expensive brooch than other tradesmen wore in their hats.

Biron said to Holofernes, "And now forward, for we have put you in countenance."

One meaning of "put you in countenance" was "encouraged you."

Holofernes replied, "You have put me out of countenance. You have disconcerted me."

Biron said, "False; we have given you faces."

Another meaning of "put you in countenance" was "have given you a face or faces."

Holofernes said, "But you have out-faced them all."

"To out-face" means "to mock" or "to put to shame."

Biron said, "Even if you were a lion, we would do so."

Boyet said, "Therefore, as he is an ass, let him go. And so adieu, sweet Jude! Why does he stay and not leave?"

Dumain said, "He is waiting for the latter end of his name."

The latter part of the name "Judas" is "ass."

Biron said, "For the ass to the Jude; give it to him — Jude-ass, away!"

He was thinking of the fable by Aesop in which an ass finds a lion skin that huntsmen are drying. The ass wears the lion skin, and all the animals are afraid when they see him until the ass brays with pleasure and so reveals that he is only an ass.

With dignity, Holofernes said, "This is not generous, not gentle, not humble."

In other words, the way you are acting is not nobly minded, not well bred, not considerate. He was accusing the lords of lacking proper etiquette and of not behaving like gentlemen.

Holofernes was correct. Boyet, Biron, Longaville, and Dumain were behaving badly.

The ladies and King Ferdinand had not joined in the mocking.

Boyet said, "A light for Monsieur Judas! It grows dark, he may stumble."

The light Biron referred to was a Judas candlestick. It had places for seven candles, but one "candle," which was made of wood and painted to resemble a candle, was called the Judas candle.

Holofernes stepped to the side.

The Princess said, "Alas, poor Maccabaeus, how he has been tormented!"

Don Adriano de Armado, costumed as Hector, stepped forward.

Biron said, "Hide your head, Achilles. Here comes Hector in arms."

Achilles was the foremost Greek warrior in the Trojan War, and Hector was the foremost Trojan warrior.

Dumain said, "Though my mocks rebound against me, I will now be merry."

King Ferdinand said, "Hector was but an ordinary Trojan, not a Trojan hero, in comparison to this man, Armado."

In this society, the word "Trojan" also meant "drinking buddy."

Boyet asked, "But is this Hector?"

King Ferdinand said, "I think Hector was not so well-built."

Possibly, King Ferdinand was trying to be genuinely complimentary as a result of the earlier mocking of Holofernes. If so, it backfired, for the other lords continued to be mocking.

Longaville said, "His leg is too big for Hector's."

Dumain said, "More calf, certainly."

In other words, Armado was more of a fool — a calf — than was Hector.

Boyet said, "No; he is best endowed in the small."

The small is the part of the leg under the calf. Boyet was saying that Armado was endowed with small things; great things belonged to the hero Hector.

Biron said, "This cannot be Hector."

Dumain said, "He's a god or a painter, for he makes faces."

Armado said, "The armipotent Mars, of lances the almighty, gave Hector a gift —"

"Armipotent" meant "powerful in the use of arms, aka weapons."

Dumain named a gift: "A gilt nutmeg."

A gilt nutmeg was a nutmeg that had been brushed with egg yolk. Such gifts were used to flavor drinks. They were also lovers' gifts.

Other members of the audience named possible gifts.

Biron said, "A lemon."

Longaville said, "A lemon stuck with cloves."

Lemons and cloves were also used to spice drinks.

Dumain said, "No, a cloven lemon."

He was punning. A "leman" is a sweetheart, and a cloven leman/lemon is metaphorically a vulva.

Armado said, "Peace! Quiet! The armipotent Mars, of lances the almighty, gave Hector a gift, the heir of Ilion."

If the gift that the war-god Mars gave Hector was an heir, then Mars cuckolded Hector.

"Ilion" was another name for "Troy."

Armado continued, "Hector was a man so strong-winded, that certainly he would fight; yes, from morning until night, out of his pavilion. I am that flower —"

Members of the audience began to name flowers.

Dumain said, "That mint."

Longaville said, "That columbine."

Mint and columbine are common, not exotic and valuable, flowers.

Armado said, "Sweet Lord Longaville, rein your tongue."

Longaville said, "I must rather give it free rein, for it runs against Hector."

Dumain said, "Yes, and Hector's a greyhound."

Some dogs were named Hector. In addition, Hector was famous for losing heart and running away from Achilles. In Homer's *Iliad*, Hector ran three times around the walls of Troy before finally facing and fighting Achilles, who killed him.

Armado said, "The sweet war-man is dead and rotten; sweet chucks, beat not the bones of the buried. When he breathed, he was a man. But I will go forward with my device, with my performance."

"Chucks" meant "dear friends."

To the Princess, Armado said, "Sweet royalty, bestow on me the sense of hearing."

In other words, please give me the satisfaction of your listening to my performance (preferably without interruptions).

The Princess replied, "Speak, brave Hector. We are much delighted."

Armado said, "I do adore thy sweet grace's slipper."

Boyet whispered to Dumain, "He loves her by the foot —"

Dumain whispered back, "He may not by the yard."

In this society, "yard" was a slang word for "penis."

Armado said, "This Hector far surmounted Hannibal —"

By "surmounted," Armado meant "surpassed." Hannibal was a Carthaginian general who crossed the Alps and terrorized the Romans.

Armado continued, "The party is gone—"

This meant, the person is dead, aka Hector is dead.

In this society, the word "gone" also meant "pregnant."

Costard said, "The party is gone, fellow Hector, she is gone; she is two months on her way to giving birth."

Armado asked, "What meanest thou?"

Costard replied, "Truly, unless you play the honest Trojan, and do the right thing by marrying her, the poor wench is cast away. She's pregnant; the child brags in her belly already. Because it brags already, we know that it is yours."

Armado, and Spaniards in general, had a reputation for bragging.

Armado replied, "Dost thou infamonize me among potentates? Thou shalt die."

"Infamonize" meant "infamize, aka defame."

Costard said, "Then shall Hector be whipped for Jaquenetta, who is pregnant by him, and hanged for Pompey, who is dead by him."

The usual punishment for fornication was whipping, and since Armado had threatened to kill Costard, who was playing Pompey, Armado would also be punished for murder.

Dumain said, "Most rare Pompey!"

Boyet said, "Renowned Pompey!"

Biron said, "Greater than great! Great, great, great Pompey! Pompey the Huge!"

Dumain said, "Hector trembles."

Biron said, "Pompey is angry. More Ates, more Ates! Stir them on! Stir them on!"

Ate was the Roman goddess of strife and discord. Here Biron was using the word "Ates" metaphorically in the sense of additional exhortations for "Pompey" and "Hector" to fight.

Dumain said, "Hector will challenge him."

Biron said, "Yes, he will, if he has no more man's blood in his belly than will sup a flea. If he has even a little courage, he will challenge him to fight."

Armado said to Costard, "By the north pole, I do challenge thee."

Costard replied, "I will not fight with a pole, like a northern man. Instead, I'll slash; I'll do it by the sword. I bepray you, let me borrow my arms again."

He was referring to the weapons he had carried when he was front and center as he played Pompey. He wanted to use the stage weapons to fight Armado.

Dumain cried, "Make room for the incensed and angry Worthies!"

Costard said, "I'll do it in my shirt."

He was so eager to fight Armado that he would fight without armor.

Dumain cried, "Most resolute Pompey!"

Mote said, "Master, let me take you a buttonhole lower."

One meaning of this was a request to Costard to allow Mote to help him take his jacket off. Another meaning was this: "Master, let me take you a peg lower."

The idiom "take down a peg or two" means to "lower someone's high opinion of himself."

Armado resisted Mote's attempt to remove his jacket.

Mote continued, "Do you not see that Pompey is uncasing — taking off some clothing — for the combat? What do you mean? You will lose your reputation."

Armado said, "Gentlemen and soldiers, pardon me; I will not combat — fight — in my shirt."

"You may not deny it," Dumain said. "Pompey has made the challenge. You must fight him."

Actually, it was Armado who had challenged Costard, who had accepted the challenge.

"Sweet bloods, I both may and will deny the fight," Armado said.

"What reason do you have for it?" Biron asked.

"The naked truth of it is, I have no shirt under my jacket," Armado said. "I go woolward for penance."

He meant that he allowed the itchy wool of his jacket to touch his naked skin as a form of penance.

Boyet said, "True, and it was enjoined him in Rome for want of linen."

In other words, yes, he does do this as a form of penance, but he is forced to because he has no shirt. Boyet was implying that Armado was too poverty stricken to have a shirt.

Boyet continued, "Since when, I'll be sworn, he wore nothing but a dishcloth of Jaquenetta's, and he wears that next to his heart for a favor, a love token."

Marcadé, one of the Princess' attendants, arrived and walked over to her and said, "God save you, madam!"

The Princess replied, "You are welcome, Marcadé, but you are interrupting our merriment."

Marcadé replied, "I am sorry, madam, for the news I bring is heavy on my tongue. The King your father —"

She knew immediately what had happened; her father had been very ill when she left France.

She said, "He is dead, for my life!"

"Yes," Marcadé said, "That is my news. My tale is told."

Marcadé's name seems to be related to Mercury, the name of the messenger of the gods. In addition, it can be split into mar-cade, or mar Arcadia. His news had ruined the happiness of King Ferdinand's park, which was usually a pleasant and quiet place of happiness like Arcadia.

"Worthies, away!" Biron ordered. "The scene begins to cloud."

Armado said, "As for mine own part, I breathe free breath."

He was happy that he had not had to fight. He was still a free man, and he was still breathing.

Armado continued, "I have seen the day of wrong through the little hole of discretion, and I will right myself like a soldier."

Armado was thinking of two proverbs: 1) One may see day at a little hole, and 2) Discretion is the better part of valor.

The first proverb meant "I am no fool." Armado has seen the day of wrong. He is no fool; he can see that he has done wrong. That wrong was to make Jaquenetta pregnant without being married to her.

The second proverb meant "It is better to avoid danger than to confront it." Armado and Costard had been about to fight because of Jaquenetta, whom Costard loved first but whom Armado made pregnant. A wise man would remove the reason for the fight, thereby preventing future fights. How to do that? Armado could do the right thing and marry Jaquenetta. Once she is married, Costard will have no reason to fight for her.

What does "I will right myself like a soldier" mean? Armado has made it clear that he does not want to fight; however, he also wants to do the right thing to save his honor as a soldier. Armado has realized his misdeed, and like an honorable soldier, he will make amends. He will marry Jaquenetta.

The Worthies exited.

King Ferdinand asked her, "How fares your majesty? How are you?"

The Princess ordered, "Boyet, prepare everything. I will go away from here tonight."

King Ferdinand requested, "Madam, do not leave tonight; I do beseech you, stay."

The Princess said again to Boyet, "Prepare everything so we can leave tonight, I say."

She then said to King Ferdinand and the other lords, "I thank you, gracious lords, for all your fair endeavors; and entreat, out of a newly sad soul, that you vouchsafe in your rich wisdom to excuse or ignore the liberal and unrestrained opposition of our spirits, if too boldly we have borne ourselves in the exchange of conversation. Your great courtesy and affability were responsible for our speaking so freely.

"Farewell, worthy lord! A heavy heart bears not a nimble tongue. Excuse me, therefore, for coming too short of thanks for my great suit to you that was so easily obtained."

The diplomatic mission the Princess had come on had been brought to a conclusion that was satisfactory to her.

King Ferdinand said, "The extreme end of time extremely forms all causes to the purpose of time's speed, and often at time's very loose decides that which long process could not arbitrate."

The "loose" is the moment at which an archer releases, aka shoots, an arrow, and it flies away.

He meant that time as it slips quickly away forces things to come to an end point, and as a period of time comes to an end, it forces people to make decisions that would not be made so quickly if more time were available. Lack of time forces decisions to be made that could not be made even after long deliberation.

He had made a decision that concerned the Princess.

King Ferdinand continued, "And though the mourning brow of progeny forbids the smiling courtesy of love the holy suit that fain it would convince, yet, since love's argument was first on foot, let not the cloud of sorrow jostle it from what it purposed; since, to wail friends and family lost is not by much so wholesome-profitable as to rejoice at friends — and family — but newly found."

He meant that although the Princess was mourning the death of her father, and although that fact forbid a smiling man who loved her to propose to her a holy suit — the King meant marriage — that he wanted to propose to her, yet since the man who loved her had loved her before her father died, she ought not to allow her sorrow to keep the lover from his purpose — which in this case is to ask her to marry him. Why? Because to mourn the loss of family and friends is not by much as beneficial to well-being as it is to rejoice because of newly found family and friends.

If the Princess were to marry him, King Ferdinand would be a new member of her family.

The phrase "not by much" is ambiguous. It could mean "a little, not a lot" or "not by a whole lot."

Once again, language proved to be slippery. Using the right words and putting them in the right order is often incredibly difficult. Understanding the sentences of other people is also often incredibly difficult.

Using archaic language in ordinary conversation is a mistake because it impedes understanding. People won't understand what you are saying.

Similarly, using archaic forms of wooing in a more modern time is a mistake because the woman the man is courting is likely to think that such wooing is a joke.

The Princess said, "I don't understand you. My griefs are double."

One grief was due to the death of her father; another grief was due to the death of her King.

But other people may have thought that her griefs were double because 1) She was mourning the loss of a loved one, and 2) She was mourning because she could not understand King Ferdinand.

Biron, who had recently learned the value of clear communication, tried to help, but he was still trying to learn to speak clearly:

"Honest plain words best pierce the ear of grief. You can understand the King by these badges."

Badges are distinguishing marks. Biron now mentioned some of those distinguishing marks, which included the foolish actions of the lords:

"For you ladies' fair sakes, we lords have neglected time and have played foul play with our oaths. We have not studied as we swore we would, but instead we have fallen in love and therefore we have broken our oaths.

"Your beauty, ladies, has much deformed us, fashioning our dispositions even to the opposite end of what we intended. Out of love for you, we have done silly things although we did not want to appear silly.

"And what in us has seemed ridiculous — as love is full of unbefitting impulses, all wanton as a child, skipping and vain, superficial and meaningless, formed by the eye and therefore, like the eye, full of strange shapes, of habits and of forms, varying in subjects as the eye rolls to every varied object in its glance. We have seemed ridiculous, but we have seemed ridiculous because we acted out of love for you.

"If this foolish presence of unrestrained love that was put on by us has — in your Heavenly eyes — been unseemly to our oaths and the serious and grave part of our character, then you should realize that those Heavenly eyes, which look upon these faults of ours, tempted us to do those foolish errors.

"Therefore, ladies, since our love is yours, the errors that love makes are likewise yours. All of the errors that we have made were made out of love for you.

"Being false once allows us to forever be true to those who make us both — fair ladies, you make us both. We have broken our vows because of you and so we have been false, but we have broken our vows so that we can always be true to you ladies.

"And even that falsehood, in itself a sin, thus purifies itself and turns to grace. Breaking our vows is a sin, but it is a sin that leads to us always being true to you. The result of our breaking our vows is a virtue that purifies the sin and turns the sin to grace."

The Princess said, "We have received your letters that are full of love, and we have received your favors, aka love tokens, which are the ambassadors of love.

"But we maidens, talking together and judging the letters and favors, thought that they were simply courtly entertainment and pleasant jests and courtesies.

"We regarded them as a pleasant way to fill up the time — like bombast and lining."

Bombast is stuffing that fills up space in a jacket. Another meaning of "bombast" is "high-flown language." "Lining" refers to the lining of clothing, and the lines in a letter.

The Princess continued, "But we have not thought of them as being any more serious than this, and therefore we have met your loves in what we thought was their own fashion — like a merriment and a joke."

The ladies had not realized that the lords were seriously in love.

Dumain said, "Our letters, madam, showed much more than jest."

Longaville said, "So did our looks."

Rosaline replied, "We did not regard them like that. We did not think that they were serious, and so we did not treat them seriously."

King Ferdinand said, "Now, at the last minute of the hour, grant us your loves."

The Princess replied, "The time we have to decide is, I think, too short to make a world-without-end — a forever — bargain in.

"No, no, my lord, your grace is much perjured because you have broken your oath. You are full of grievous — yet dear — guiltiness; and therefore I say this to you:

"If for my love — and I don't see why you should do this — you will do anything, I have something you can do for me.

"I will not trust your oath, so you need not swear to do this, but go speedily to some forlorn and austere hermitage, remote from all the pleasures of the world.

"There stay until the twelve celestial signs have brought about the annual reckoning of the passage of one year.

"If this austere unsociable life does not make you change the offer of marriage you made in the heat of your blood, and if frosts and fasts, hard lodging and thin clothing do not nip the gaudy blossoms of your love, but if your love for me instead endures this trial and your love lasts, then, at the expiration of the year, come and claim me, claim my hand in marriage with you by virtue of these things you have done to deserve me."

She held his hand and said, "And, by this virgin palm now kissing your hand, I will be your wife; and until that instant I will shut my woeful self up in a mourning house, raining the tears of lamentation in remembrance of my father's death.

"If you are unwilling to do what I request, then let our hands part, and neither of us will be entitled to the other's heart."

Still holding her hand, King Ferdinand replied, "If I would be unwilling to do this, or to do more than this, in order to pamper these faculties of mine with rest, may the sudden hand of death close my eyes!

"I will go and be a hermit — my heart is in your breast."

King Ferdinand of Navarre and the Princess of France talked quietly together.

Dumain said to Katherine, "What will you give to me, my love? What will you give to me? A wife?"

Katherine replied, "A beard, fair health, and honesty; with three-fold love I wish you all these three."

Dumain said, "Shall I say, 'I thank you, gentle wife'?"

"No, my lord," Katherine said. "For a twelvemonth and a day, I'll pay no attention to words that smooth-faced wooers say. Come to me when the King comes to my lady. Then, if I have much love, I'll give you some."

"I'll serve you truly and faithfully until then," Dumain said.

"Do not swear to do that, lest you be forsworn again," Katherine said.

Dumain and Katherine talked quietly together.

"What says Maria?" Longaville asked.

His offer of marriage was implicit.

Maria replied, "At the twelvemonth's end, I'll change my black gown for a faithful lover."

"I'll wait with patience, but the time is long," Longaville said.

"The time is much like you," Maria said. "You are long in your name, and few men who are taller than you are as young as you."

Longaville and Maria talked quietly together.

Biron said to Rosaline, "Are you deep in thought, my lady? My lady, look at me. Behold the windows of my heart, my eyes. Look at the humble wooer who awaits your answer there. Impose some service on me so that I can earn your love."

"Often have I heard about you, my Lord Biron, before I saw you, and the world's large tongue, which gossips freely, proclaims you to be a man replete with mocking, full of unflattering comparisons and wounding jeers, which you will execute on all people of all ranks who lie within the mercy of your wit.

"To weed this bitter wormwood from your fruitful brain, and therewithal to win me, if you please — because without the weeding of the wormwood I am not to be won — you shall this twelvemonth term from day to day visit the speechless sick and continually converse with groaning wretches; and your task shall be, with all the fierce endeavor of your wit to make the tormented helpless people smile."

"You want me to arouse wild laughter in the throat of death?" Biron asked. "It cannot be done; it is impossible: Mirth cannot move a soul that is in agony."

Rosaline replied, "Why, that's the way to choke a taunting, scoffing spirit, whose influence is begotten by that easy-going indulgence that shallow, laughing hearers give to fools.

"A jest's prosperity lies in the ear of him who hears it, never in the tongue of him who makes it. So then, if sickly ears, deafened with the clamors of their own dire groans, will hear your idle scorns, then continue to make them, and I will have you and your fault as well, but if they will not, then throw away that mocking spirit, and I shall find you empty of that fault, and I will be joyful about your reformation."

Rosaline had seen and heard Biron's mocking spirit in abundance during the attempted performance of the Worthies. She had not liked what she had seen and heard.

"A twelvemonth! A year!" Biron said. "Well, befall what will befall, come what may, I'll jest for a twelvemonth in a hospital."

The Princess of France said to King Ferdinand, "Yes, my sweet lord, and so I take my leave."

King Ferdinand said, "No, madam. We will accompany you on your way."

Biron said, "Our wooing does not end like an old comic play. Jack has not Jill. These ladies' good manners might well have made our sport a comedy. All they had to do was to marry us."

King Ferdinand said, "Come, sir, the happy ending lacks only a twelvemonth and a day, and then it will end as it should."

"That's too long for a play," Biron said.

Don Adriano de Armado walked over to the group and said to the King, "Sweet majesty, vouchsafe me —"

The Princess of France asked, "Isn't he the man who played Hector?"

Dumain affirmed, "Yes, the worthy knight of Troy."

Armado said to the King, "I will kiss thy royal finger, and then take my leave. I am a votary; I have vowed to Jaquenetta to hold the plow for her sweet love three years."

"To hold the plow" means "to be a farmer." A farmer holds the plow to guide and direct it to go where it should go.

The bawdy meaning of the phrase used the word "plow" as a noun; Armado's "plow" was located a few inches under his bellybutton. Armado would hold his plow to guide it to where it would hit its target: Jaquenetta's vagina.

But "hold" has a secondary meaning. It can be used in "hold back" or "withhold." It can mean "'hold." A proverb stated, "He who holds the plow reaps no corn." In other words, he who does not plow reaps no crop.

The bawdy meaning of this is "He who withholds and does not use his penis reaps no infant."

Possibly, Jaquenetta did not want to get pregnant a second time for at least three years.

Armado continued, "But, most esteemed greatness, will you hear the dialogue that the two learned men Holofernes and Sir Nathaniel have created in praise of the owl and the cuckoo? It should have followed the end of our show."

King Ferdinand said, "Call them forth quickly; we will do so."

Armado called, "Ho! Come here!"

Holofernes, Sir Nathaniel, Mote, Costard, and others approached and separated into two groups.

Armado said, "This side is *Hiems*, aka Winter, and this side is *Ver*, the Spring. The one is defended by the owl, the other by the cuckoo.

"*Hiems*" is Latin for "winter," and "*ver*" is Latin for "spring."

"*Ver*, begin."

The people on the side representing Spring sang this song:

"*When daisies pied and violets blue*"

The daisies were "pied" — they were multi-colored.

"*And lady-smocks all silver-white*"

Lady-smocks are cuckoo-flowers.

"*And cuckoo-buds of yellow hue*

"*Do paint the meadows with delight,*

"*The cuckoo then, on every tree,*

"*Mocks married men; for thus sings he, 'Cuckoo;*

"*'Cuckoo, cuckoo.' Oh, word of fear,*

"*Unpleasing to a married ear!*"

Cuckoo birds lay their eggs in the nests of other birds, and so they call to mind cuckolds. "Cuckoo" is a word of fear to married men because "cuckoo" sounds like "cuckold."

"When shepherds pipe on oaten straws"

The shepherds' wind instruments are made from the straw — dried stalks — of oats.

"And merry larks are plowmen's clocks,"

Larks sing in the early morning, when plowmen get up. Plowmen rise with the morning lark.

"When turtles tread, and rooks, and daws,"

The phrase "When turtles tread" means "When turtledoves mate." "Daws" are the birds also known as "jackdaws."

"And maidens bleach their summer smocks"

The young virgins bleach their summer smocks in the sunshine as they prepare to look their best in order to get boyfriends.

"The cuckoo then, on every tree,

"Mocks married men; for thus sings he, 'Cuckoo;

"'Cuckoo, cuckoo.' Oh, word of fear,

"Unpleasing to a married ear!"

Then the people on the side representing Winter sang this song:

"When icicles hang by the wall

"And Dick the shepherd blows his nail"

Dick blows on his fingernails to keep his hands warm in the winter.

"And Tom bears logs into the hall

"And milk comes frozen home in pail,

"When blood is nipped and ways be foul,

The ways — roads — are foul because of snow and ice.

"Then nightly sings the staring owl, 'Tu-whit;

"'Tu-who,' a merry note,"

"Tu-whit; tu-who" can be understood as "to it; to woo." "To it" can mean "go to it" or "to have sex."

"While greasy Joan doth keel the pot."

"Keel" means to "cool." Joan would stir the pot to cool the liquid and keep it from boiling over.

"When all aloud the wind doth blow

"And coughing drowns the parson's saw"

A "saw" is a "wise saying or platitude." Coughing drowns out the parson's words.

"And birds sit brooding in the snow

"And Marian's nose looks red and raw,

"When roasted crabs hiss in the bowl,"

The roasted crabs are crabapples that have been placed in a bowl of warmed ale or wine.

"Then nightly sings the staring owl, 'Tu-whit;

"'Tu-who,' a merry note,

"While greasy Joan doth keel the pot."

Armado then said, "The words of Mercury are harsh after the songs of Apollo."

He meant that prose would ruin the mood created by the pleasing verse of the two songs. Mercury was the messenger of the gods, and so his words concerned serious business. Apollo was the god of music and the words of his songs were entertaining.

Armado then said to the readers of this book: "You go your way; we characters in this book will go our way. And so farewell."

APPENDIX A: NOTES

The following lines are thought to be a first draft of some lines that appear in Biron's long speech near the end of Act 4, scene 3:

> And where that you have vow'd to study, lords,
> In that each of you have forsworn his book,
> Can you still dream and pore and thereon look?
> For when would you, my lord, or you, or you,
> Have found the ground of study's excellence
> Without the beauty of a woman's face?
> *From women's eyes this doctrine I derive;*
> *They are the ground, the books, the academes*
> *From whence doth spring the true Promethean fire*
> Why, universal plodding poisons up
> The nimble spirits in the arteries,
> As motion and long-during action tires
> The sinewy vigor of the traveller.
> Now, for not looking on a woman's face,
> You have in that forsworn the use of eyes
> And study too, the causer of your vow;
> For where is any author in the world
> Teaches such beauty as a woman's eye?
> Learning is but an adjunct to ourself
> And where we are our learning likewise is:
> Then when ourselves we see in ladies' eyes,
> Do we not likewise see our learning there?

***

For more information about King Pepin the Short, Bellysant, and Valentine and Orson, see this book:

John Ashton, *Romances of Chivalry*. T. Fisher Unwin, 1887. 235-256.
Free download:
https://archive.org/details/romanceschivalr01ashtgoog

APPENDIX B: ABOUT THE AUTHOR

It was a dark and stormy night. Suddenly a cry rang out, and on a hot summer night in 1954, Josephine, wife of Carl Bruce, gave birth to a boy — me. Unfortunately, this young married couple allowed Reuben Saturday, Josephine's brother, to name their first-born. Reuben, aka "The Joker," decided that Bruce was a nice name, so he decided to name me Bruce Bruce. I have gone by my middle name — David — ever since.

Being named Bruce David Bruce hasn't been all bad. Bank tellers remember me very quickly, so I don't often have to show an ID. It can be fun in charades, also. When I was a counselor as a teenager at Camp Echoing Hills in Warsaw, Ohio, a fellow counselor gave the signs for "sounds like" and "two words," then she pointed to a bruise on her leg twice. Bruise Bruise? Oh yeah, Bruce Bruce is the answer!

Uncle Reuben, by the way, gave me a haircut when I was in kindergarten. He cut my hair short and shaved a small bald spot on the back of my head. My mother wouldn't let me go to school until the bald spot grew out again.

Of all my brothers and sisters (six in all), I am the only transplant to Athens, Ohio. I was born in Newark, Ohio, and have lived all around Southeastern Ohio. However, I moved to Athens to go to Ohio University and have never left.

At Ohio U, I never could make up my mind whether to major in English or Philosophy, so I got a Bachelor's with a double major in both areas in 1980, then I added a Master's in English in 1984 and a Master's in Philosophy in 1985. Currently, I am a retired English instructor at Ohio U.

If all goes well, I will publish one or two books a year for the rest of my life. (On the other hand, a good way to make God laugh is to tell Her your plans.)

By the way, my sister Brenda Kennedy writes romances such as *A New Beginning* and *Shattered Dreams*.

APPENDIX C: SOME BOOKS BY DAVID BRUCE

Retellings of a Classic Work of Literature

Arden of Faversham: A Retelling

Ben Jonson's The Alchemist: *A Retelling*

Ben Jonson's The Arraignment, or Poetaster: *A Retelling*

Ben Jonson's Bartholomew Fair: *A Retelling*

Ben Jonson's The Case is Altered: *A Retelling*

Ben Jonson's Catiline's Conspiracy: *A Retelling*

Ben Jonson's The Devil is an Ass: *A Retelling*

Ben Jonson's Epicene: *A Retelling*

Ben Jonson's Every Man in His Humor: *A Retelling*

Ben Jonson's Every Man Out of His Humor: *A Retelling*

Ben Jonson's The Fountain of Self-Love, or Cynthia's Revels: *A Retelling*

Ben Jonson's The Magnetic Lady, or Humors Reconciled: *A Retelling*

Ben Jonson's The New Inn, or The Light Heart: *A Retelling*

Ben Jonson's Sejanus' Fall: *A Retelling*

Ben Jonson's The Staple of News: *A Retelling*

Ben Jonson's A Tale of a Tub: *A Retelling*

Ben Jonson's Volpone, or the Fox: *A Retelling*

Christopher Marlowe's Complete Plays: Retellings

Christopher Marlowe's Dido, Queen of Carthage: *A Retelling*

Christopher Marlowe's Doctor Faustus: *Retellings of the 1604 A-Text and of the 1616 B-Text*

Christopher Marlowe's Edward II: *A Retelling*

Christopher Marlowe's The Massacre at Paris: *A Retelling*

Christopher Marlowe's The Rich Jew of Malta: *A Retelling*

Christopher Marlowe's Tamburlaine, Parts 1 and 2: *Retellings*

Dante's Divine Comedy: *A Retelling in Prose*

Dante's Inferno: *A Retelling in Prose*

Dante's Purgatory: *A Retelling in Prose*

Dante's Paradise: *A Retelling in Prose*

The Famous Victories of Henry V: A Retelling

From the Iliad *to the* Odyssey: *A Retelling in Prose of Quintus of Smyrna's* Posthomerica

George Chapman, Ben Jonson, and John Marston's Eastward Ho! *A Retelling*

George Peele's The Arraignment of Paris: *A Retelling*

George Peele's The Battle of Alcazar: *A Retelling*

George Peele's David and Bathsheba, and the Tragedy of Absalom: *A Retelling*

George Peele's Edward I: *A Retelling*

George Peele's The Old Wives' Tale: *A Retelling*

George-a-Greene: *A Retelling*

The History of King Leir: *A Retelling*

Homer's Iliad: *A Retelling in Prose*

Homer's Odyssey: *A Retelling in Prose*

J.W. Gent.'s The Valiant Scot: *A Retelling*

Jason and the Argonauts: A Retelling in Prose of Apollonius of Rhodes' Argonautica

John Ford: Eight Plays Translated into Modern English

John Ford's The Broken Heart: *A Retelling*

John Ford's The Fancies, Chaste and Noble: *A Retelling*

John Ford's The Lady's Trial: *A Retelling*

John Ford's The Lover's Melancholy: *A Retelling*

John Ford's Love's Sacrifice: *A Retelling*

John Ford's Perkin Warbeck: *A Retelling*

John Ford's The Queen: *A Retelling*

John Ford's 'Tis Pity She's a Whore: *A Retelling*

John Lyly's Campaspe: *A Retelling*

John Lyly's Endymion, The Man in the Moon: *A Retelling*

John Lyly's Galatea: *A Retelling*

John Lyly's Love's Metamorphosis: *A Retelling*

John Lyly's Midas: *A Retelling*

John Lyly's Mother Bombie: *A Retelling*

John Lyly's Sappho and Phao: *A Retelling*

John Lyly's The Woman in the Moon: *A Retelling*

John Webster's The White Devil: *A Retelling*

King Edward III: *A Retelling*

Mankind: *A Medieval Morality Play* (A Retelling)

Margaret Cavendish's The Unnatural Tragedy: *A Retelling*

The Merry Devil of Edmonton: *A Retelling*

The Summoning of Everyman: *A Medieval Morality Play* (A Retelling)

Robert Greene's Friar Bacon and Friar Bungay: *A Retelling*

The Taming of a Shrew: *A Retelling*

Tarlton's Jests: A Retelling

Thomas Middleton's A Chaste Maid in Cheapside: *A Retelling*

Thomas Middleton's Women Beware Women: *A Retelling*

Thomas Middleton and Thomas Dekker's The Roaring Girl: *A Retelling*

Thomas Middleton and William Rowley's The Changeling: *A Retelling*

The Trojan War and Its Aftermath: Four Ancient Epic Poems

Virgil's Aeneid: *A Retelling in Prose*

William Shakespeare's 5 Late Romances: Retellings in Prose

William Shakespeare's 10 Histories: Retellings in Prose

William Shakespeare's 11 Tragedies: Retellings in Prose

William Shakespeare's 12 Comedies: Retellings in Prose

William Shakespeare's 38 Plays: Retellings in Prose
William Shakespeare's 1 Henry IV, aka Henry IV, Part 1: *A Retelling in Prose*
William Shakespeare's 2 Henry IV, aka Henry IV, Part 2: *A Retelling in Prose*
William Shakespeare's 1 Henry VI, aka Henry VI, Part 1: *A Retelling in Prose*
William Shakespeare's 2 Henry VI, aka Henry VI, Part 2: *A Retelling in Prose*
William Shakespeare's 3 Henry VI, aka Henry VI, Part 3: *A Retelling in Prose*
William Shakespeare's All's Well that Ends Well: *A Retelling in Prose*
William Shakespeare's Antony and Cleopatra: *A Retelling in Prose*
William Shakespeare's As You Like It: *A Retelling in Prose*
William Shakespeare's The Comedy of Errors: *A Retelling in Prose*
William Shakespeare's Coriolanus: *A Retelling in Prose*
William Shakespeare's Cymbeline: A Retelling in Prose
William Shakespeare's Hamlet: A Retelling in Prose
William Shakespeare's Henry V: A Retelling in Prose
William Shakespeare's Henry VIII: A Retelling in Prose
William Shakespeare's Julius Caesar: A Retelling in Prose
William Shakespeare's King John: A Retelling in Prose
William Shakespeare's King Lear: *A Retelling in Prose*
William Shakespeare's Love's Labor's Lost: *A Retelling in Prose*
William Shakespeare's Macbeth: *A Retelling in Prose*
William Shakespeare's Measure for Measure: *A Retelling in Prose*
William Shakespeare's The Merchant of Venice: *A Retelling in Prose*
William Shakespeare's The Merry Wives of Windsor: *A Retelling in Prose*
William Shakespeare's A Midsummer Night's Dream: *A Retelling in Prose*
William Shakespeare's Much Ado About Nothing: *A Retelling in Prose*
William Shakespeare's Othello: *A Retelling in Prose*
William Shakespeare's Pericles, Prince of Tyre: *A Retelling in Prose*
William Shakespeare's Richard II: *A Retelling in Prose*
William Shakespeare's Richard III: *A Retelling in Prose*
William Shakespeare's Romeo and Juliet: *A Retelling in Prose*
William Shakespeare's The Taming of the Shrew: *A Retelling in Prose*
William Shakespeare's The Tempest: *A Retelling in Prose*
William Shakespeare's Timon of Athens: *A Retelling in Prose*
William Shakespeare's Titus Andronicus: *A Retelling in Prose*
William Shakespeare's Troilus and Cressida: *A Retelling in Prose*
William Shakespeare's Twelfth Night: *A Retelling in Prose*
William Shakespeare's The Two Gentlemen of Verona: *A Retelling in Prose*
William Shakespeare's The Two Noble Kinsmen: *A Retelling in Prose*
William Shakespeare's The Winter's Tale: *A Retelling in Prose*